THE MYSTERIOUS SHIN SHIRA

A short distance beyond lay a terrible dragon

George Edward Farrow
AUTHOR OF
The WALLYPUG of WHY

THE MYSTERIOUS SHIN SHIRA

Illustrated
W. G. Easton

Copyright © 2008 BiblioBazaar
All rights reserved

THE MYSTERIOUS
SHIN SHIRA

CONTENTS

MYSTERY NO. I 11
  SHIN SHIRA APPEARS

MYSTERY NO. II 20
  SHIN SHIRA AND THE DRAGON

MYSTERY NO. III 26
  THE MAGIC CARPET

MYSTERY NO. IV 37
  SHIN SHIRA AND THE DUCHESS

MYSTERY NO. V 47
  SHIN SHIRA AND THE LAME DUCK

MYSTERY NO. VI 57
  SHIN SHIRA AND THE DIAMOND

MYSTERY NO. VII 69
  SHIN SHIRA AND THE ROC

MYSTERY NO. VIII 80
  SHIN SHIRA AND THE MAD BULL

MYSTERY NO. IX 90
  SHIN SHIRA AND THE QUEEN OF HEARTS

MYSTERY NO. X AND LAST 101
  SHIN SHIRA DISAPPEARS

LIST OF ILLUSTRATIONS

"A SHORT DISTANCE BEYOND LAY A TERRIBLE DRAGON" 2

"THE EXECUTIONER IN HIS AGITATION DROPPED HIS AXE" 18

"WE FLOATED AWAY OVER THE ROOFS OF THE HOUSES" 30

"SHIN SHIRA PLACED THEM IN THE CRYSTAL BOWL" 42

"HIS PINIONS WERE STRONG AND MIGHTY" 76

"THIS WAS CAREFULLY SET BEFORE THE KING" 95

MYSTERY NO. I

SHIN SHIRA APPEARS

It was very remarkable how I first came to make his acquaintance at all. Shin Shira I mean. I had been sitting at my desk, writing, for quite a long time, when suddenly I heard, as I thought, a noise in another part of the room. I turned my head hastily and looked towards the door, but it was fast closed and there was apparently nobody in the room but myself.

"Strange!" I murmured, looking about to try and discover what had caused the sound, and then my eyes lighted, to my great surprise, upon a pair of bright yellow morocco shoes with very long, pointed toes, standing on the floor in front of a favourite little squat chair of mine which I call "the Toad."

I gazed at the yellow shoes in amazement, for they certainly did not belong to me, and they had decidedly not been there a short time before, for I had been sitting in the chair myself.

I had just got up to examine them, when, to my utter astonishment, I saw a pair of yellow stockings appearing above them; an instant later, a little yellow body; and finally, the quaintest little head that I have ever seen, surmounted by a yellow turban, in the front of which a large jewel sparkled and shone.

It was not the turban, however, but the face beneath it which claimed my greatest attention, for the eyes were nearly starting out of the head with fright, and the expression was one of the greatest anxiety.

It gave way, however, to reassurance and content directly the little man had given a hurried glance round the room, and he sank comfortably down into "the Toad" with a sigh of relief.

"Phew!" he exclaimed, drawing out a little yellow fan from his sleeve and fanning himself vigorously, "that *was* a narrow squeak! I really don't think that I've been in such a tight corner before for two hundred years at least." And he tucked his fan away again and beamed upon me complacently.

I was so astounded at the sudden appearance of this remarkable little personage that for the moment I quite lost the use of my tongue; and in the meantime my little visitor was glancing about the room with piercing eyes that seemed to take in everything.

"H'm!—writer, I suppose?" he said, nodding his head towards my desk, which was as usual littered with papers. "What line? You don't look very clever," and he glanced at me critically from under his bushy eyebrows.

"I only write books for children," I answered, "and one doesn't have to be very clever to do that."

"Oh, children!" said the little Yellow Dwarf—as I had begun to call him in my own mind. "No, you don't have to be *clever*, but you have to be—er—by the way, do you write fairy stories?" he interrupted himself to ask.

"Sometimes," I answered.

"Ah! then I can put you up to a thing or two. I'm partly a fairy myself.

"You see, it's this way," he went on hastily, seeing, I suppose, that I looked somewhat surprised at this unexpected piece of information. "Some hundreds of years ago—oh! ever so many—long before the present Japanese Empire was founded, in fact, there was a man named Shin Shira Scaramanga Manousa Yama Hawa—"

"Good gracious!" I exclaimed.

"Don't interrupt," said the little Yellow Dwarf, "it's rude, and besides, you make me forget—I can't even think now what the rest of the gentleman's name was—but anyhow, he was an ancestor of mine, and that much of his name belongs to me."

"How much?" I inquired.

"Shin Shira Scaramanga Manousa Yama Hawa," repeated the Yellow Dwarf; "but you needn't say it all," he added hastily, seeing, I suppose, that I looked rather distressed, "Shin Shira will do; in fact, that's what I am always called. Well, to continue. This ancestor of mine, part of whose name I bear, did something or other to offend his great-grandmother, who was a very influential sort of a fairy—I *could* tell you the whole story, but it's a very long one and I'll have to tell you that another time—and she was so angry with him that she condemned him to appear or disappear whenever she liked and at whatever time or place that she chose, for ever."

"For ever?" I inquired incredulously.

"Why not?" asked Shin Shira. "Fairies, you know, are immortal, and my ancestor had fairy blood in his veins. Well, to make a long story short, the spell, or whatever you choose to call it, which his great-grandmother cast over him, didn't work in him, nor in his son, nor even in his grandson; but several hundreds of years afterwards *I* was born, and then it suddenly took effect, and I have always been afflicted with the exceedingly uncomfortable misfortune of having to appear or disappear whenever the old lady likes, and in whatever place she chooses.

"It's terribly awkward at times, for one minute I may be in China taking tea with a Mandarin of the Blue Button, and have to disappear suddenly, turning up a minute later in a first-class carriage on the Underground Railway, greatly to the surprise and indignation of the passengers, especially if it happens to be overcrowded without me, as it very often is.

"Not but what it has its advantages too," he added thoughtfully, "and this very power of being able to disappear suddenly has just got me out of a most serious dilemma."

"Won't you tell me about it?" I inquired with considerable curiosity, for I was beginning to be very interested in this singular little person's account of himself.

"With pleasure," said Shin Shira; and settling himself more comfortably in "the Toad," resting his elbows on the arms of the chair, and placing the tips of his fingers together, he told me the following story.

"The very last place in which I appeared before turning up here, was in the grounds of the Palace belonging to the Grand Panjandrum—"

"Where is that situated, if you please?" I ventured to inquire.

Shin Shira gave me a quick glance.

"Do you mean to say that you actually don't even know where the land of the Grand Panjandrum is?" he asked. "H'm! well," he continued as I shook my head, "I remarked a short time ago that you didn't *look* very clever, but really, I couldn't have believed that you were so ignorant as all that. You'd better look it up in your atlas when I am gone, I can't bother to explain where it is now—but to resume my story. I appeared there, as I said, and in the middle of the kitchen garden all amongst the cabbages and beans.

"I could at first see nobody about, but at last I heard somebody singing, and presently came upon a man carrying a basket in which were some cabbages that he had evidently just gathered.

"Although he was singing so cheerfully, his head was bound up with a handkerchief, and I could see that his face was badly swollen.

"When he had come a little nearer, I bowed politely and inquired of him what place it was, for my surroundings were quite strange to me, it being my first visit to the neighbourhood.

"He told me where I was, and explained that he was the Grand Panjandrum's Chief Cook, and that he had been to gather cabbages to make an apple pie with."

I was about to ask how this was possible, when I caught Shin Shira's eye, and I could see by the light in it that he was expecting me to make some inquiry; but I was determined that he should not again have the opportunity of remarking upon my ignorance, so I held my tongue and said nothing, as though gathering cabbages in order to make an apple pie was the most natural thing in the world to do.

He waited for a moment and then continued—

"I stood talking to the man for some time, and at last I asked what was the matter with his face.

"'I've the toothache,' he said ruefully, 'and that's why I was singing; I'm told that it's a capital remedy.'

"'I'll see if I can't find a better one,' said I, taking up this little book, which I always carry with me." And Shin Shira held out for my inspection a tiny volume bound in yellow leather, with golden clasps, which was attached to his girdle by a long golden chain.

"This," he explained, "is a very remarkable book, and has been in our family for many hundreds of years. It contains directions what to do in any difficulty whatsoever, with the aid of the fairy power, which, as I have told you, I inherit from my fairy ancestor.

"The only difficulty is that, as I am partly a mortal, *sometimes* (owing perhaps to my fairy great-great-great-grandmother being in a bad temper at the moment) the fairy spell refuses to work, and then I am left in the lurch.

"This time, however, it worked splendidly, for I had only to turn to the word 'Toothache' to discover that the fairy remedy was to 'rub the *other* side of the face with a stinging nettle, and the pain and swelling would instantly disappear.'

"Fortunately there were plenty of nettles to be found in a neglected corner of the garden, and I quickly applied the remedy, which worked, as the saying is, 'like magic,' for the Grand Panjandrum's Chief Cook's face resumed its normal size at once, and the pain vanished immediately.

"It is needless to say that he was very grateful, and we were walking back to the Palace, where he had just promised to regale me with some of the choicest viands in his larder, when we met, coming towards us, a most doleful-looking individual, clothed in black and wearing a most woebegone visage.

"'It's the Court Physician,' said the Cook; 'I wonder why he is looking so melancholy. May I venture to ask, sir,' he inquired respectfully, 'the occasion of your sorrow?'

"'I am to be executed to-morrow by the Grand Panjandrum's order,' said the Court Physician dolefully, wiping a tear of self-pity from his eye.

"The Chief Cook shrugged his shoulders. 'H'm!' said he, 'if *that's* the case, and His Supreme Importance has ordered your execution, nobody can possibly prevent it, and there is nothing left but to grin and bear it.'

"'No,' said the Court Physician indignantly. 'I may have to bear it, but I shall *not* grin. I absolutely refuse! They can't do more than kill me, and I *won't* grin, so there!'

"The Chief Cook looked horrified. 'It's one of the laws of the land,' he said, 'that whenever one suffers anything at the hands of the Grand Panjandrum, one must grin and bear it; it's a most terrible offence not to do so.'

"'I don't care,' said the Court Physician recklessly, 'I shan't grin, and there's an end of it.'

"'Why are you sentenced to death?' I asked.

"'His Supreme Importance, the Grand Panjandrum, has had the toothache for three days, and I have been unable to subdue it without drawing the tooth, which His Supreme Importance refuses to permit me to do, and in a fit of temper yesterday he said that if he were not better to-day I should be executed to-morrow—and it's worse.'

"The Chief Cook looked at me delightedly.

"'If *that's* all,' he said, 'this gentleman, whose name I am unfortunately unacquainted with, has a remedy which will soon get you out of your trouble, and I shouldn't wonder if, after all, His Supreme Importance's toothache were the means of raising us all to honour and distinction;' and he proceeded to tell the Court Physician how I had been successful in ridding *him* of the toothache.

"The Court Physician was greatly interested, and after I had read to him the directions in the book, he suggested that he should take me to the Palace at once and into the presence of the Grand Panjandrum.

"'For no doubt the operation must be performed by yourself, since you alone possess the fairy power,' said he. And so we made the best of our way to the beautiful building which I could see in the distance.

"I wish I could describe to you the magnificence of that marvellous place. The jewelled windows and golden staircase; the wonderful velvety carpets and silken hangings; the hundreds of silent servants dressed in the beautiful royal livery of the Grand Panjandrum, who flitted about executing immediately the slightest wish echoed in that wonderful place.

"But it is sufficient to say that, after a lot of ceremony, I was at last ushered into the presence of the Grand Panjandrum himself.

"It is forbidden to anyone, under the most awful penalties, to describe His Supreme Importance's appearance, so I cannot tell you what he was like; but I found him suffering the most excruciating agony with the toothache, and with his face even more swollen than the Chief Cook's had been.

"At a sign from the Court Physician I quickly prepared my nettle leaves, which we had thought to gather on our way to the palace, and began to rub them gently on the Grand Panjandrum's cheek, on the opposite side of his face to that which was swollen.

"To my horror and amazement, they had no effect whatever, except immediately to raise a terrible rash upon His Supreme Importance's cheek, and to cause him such pain that he called out angrily that it was worse than the toothache itself.

"I hurriedly and anxiously consulted my little book to see if by any mischance I had failed in carrying out any of the directions; but no, there it was in black and white—'rub the *other* side with a stinging nettle.'

"I showed it to the Court Physician, and he said—

"'Try the "other" side, then: you've rubbed one side, try the other.'

"So in fear and trembling I begged His Supreme Importance's permission to apply the remedy to his other cheek, and after some demur he agreed, but making it a condition that if it failed to act I was to be immediately beheaded.

"You may imagine with what anxiety I awaited the result of my experiment, and how carefully I rubbed the nettles on.

"It was all in vain: the rash spread under the nettles and the swelling grew greater than ever—evidently my fairy power refused to work—and the Grand Panjandrum was in a fearful rage.

"'Fetch the Executioner!' he cried, in terrible tones. 'I will see this impostor executed before my eyes!' And twenty slaves flew to obey his command.

"'Grin!' whispered the Court Physician behind his hand, 'grin and bear it; it's the only thing to be done.'

"The Executioner in his agitation dropped his axe."

"I gave him a wrathful glance, and was about to speak, when at a sign from the Grand Panjandrum, two powerful slaves sprang forward and bound and gagged me.

"There was a sound of approaching footsteps, and from another entrance the Executioner appeared, followed by some slaves carrying the block.

"I thought my last moment had arrived, but just then, to my intense delight, I felt a curious sensation, which told me that I was about to disappear.

"My feet went first (this is not always the case), and then my legs, and I could see the amazement with which the Grand Panjandrum and all the assembled company were regarding the, to them, extraordinary phenomenon.

"The Executioner in his agitation dropped his axe, and stood open-mouthed regarding what was left of me; and, although I was rather anxious lest they should make an attempt to chop off my head before it finally disappeared, I managed despite my gag to 'grin' in the Grand Panjandrum's face, and an instant later I found myself here."

Shin Shira, having finished his story, drew his little fan from his sleeve and sat fanning himself with great composure, while he regarded my doubtless astonished face with considerable amusement.

"I—I'll put that story down at once, if you don't mind," I stammered, hurrying to my desk and getting out some papers.

The drawer stuck, and it was some seconds before I could get it open, and when I turned round again, to my great dismay, Shin Shira had almost disappeared.

The little yellow shoes were still there and part of a stocking, but even as I watched them they too disappeared, the long pointed toes of the shoes waggling a kind of farewell—or so I thought—and my strange little visitor had vanished.

* * * * *

MYSTERY NO. II

SHIN SHIRA AND THE DRAGON

It was during my holidays in Cornwall that I next met Shin Shira.

I had ridden by motor-car from Helston to the Lizard, and after scrambling over rugged cliffs for some time, following the white stones put by the coastguards to mark the way, I found myself at last at the most beautiful little bay imaginable, called Kynance Cove.

The tide was low, and from the glittering white sands, tall jagged rocks rose up, covered with coloured seaweed; which, together with the deep blue and green of the sky and sea, made a perfect feast of colour for the eyes.

On the shore I met an amiable young guide, who, for sixpence, undertook to show me some caves in the rocks which are not generally discovered by visitors.

They were very fine caves, one of them being called The Princess's Parlour; and while we were exploring this, I suddenly heard a roar as of some mighty animal in terrible pain.

I turned to the guide with, I expect, rather a white face, for an explanation.

He smiled at my alarm, however, and told me that it was "only the Bellows," and suggested a visit to the spot whence the sound proceeded.

We scrambled out of the cave and descended to the sands again, and passing behind a tall rock called The Tower, we saw a curious sight.

From between two enormous boulders came at intervals a great cloud of fine spray, which puffed up into the air for about twenty feet, accompanied by the roaring noise that I had previously noticed. My young guide explained to me that the noise and the spray were caused by the air in the hollow between the two boulders being forcibly expelled through a narrow slit in the rocks as each wave of the incoming tide entered. Having made this quite clear to me, he took his departure, warning me not to remain too long on the sands, as the tide was coming in rather rapidly.

I sat for some time alone on the rocks, gazing with fascinated interest at the curious effect produced by the clouds of spray coming from "the Bellows," and was at last just turning to go when I started in surprise, for there, sitting on another rock just behind me, was the little Yellow Dwarf, Shin Shira, energetically fanning himself with the little yellow fan which I had noticed at our previous meeting.

"Oh! it's you, is it?" he remarked, when he caught sight of my face. "I thought I recognised the back view; you see it was the last I saw of you when I paid you that visit in your study."

21

"And disappeared so very suddenly," I answered, going up and offering my hand, for I was very pleased to see the little man again.

"I was *obliged* to. You know of my unfortunate affliction in having to appear or disappear whenever my fairy great-great-great-grandmother wishes. *He's* safe enough, isn't he?" he added, inconsequently nodding his head towards "the Bellows."

"Who is? What do you mean?" I inquired.

"The dragon, of course," said Shin Shira.

"The dragon!" I exclaimed.

"Certainly—you know that there's a dragon imprisoned behind those rocks, don't you?"

I laughed.

"No," I said, "although I must admit that I was at first inclined to think that something of the sort was concealed there. I've had it all explained to me, though," and I proceeded to inform him of what the guide had told me concerning the matter.

"Pooh! Rubbish! He doesn't know what he's talking about," said Shin Shira contemptuously; "I'll tell you the real story of those rocks as it occurred, let's see—about eight or nine hundred years ago. I remember it quite well, for it was one of those occasions when I was *most* distressed at having to disappear at what was for me the very worst possible moment."

I settled myself comfortably on the rocks beside Shin Shira and prepared to listen with great interest.

"Let's think for a moment," said the little Yellow Dwarf, looking about him.

"It began—oh, yes! I know now. In that cave over yonder—I was eight or nine hundred years younger then, and a very warm-blooded and impressionable young fellow at that time; and I can remember being struck with the extreme beauty of the charming Princess whom I discovered in tears there when I suddenly appeared.

"The cave itself was hung about with the most beautiful silken curtains and tapestries, and on the floor were spread rugs and carpets and cushions of Oriental magnificence. Tiny tables, inlaid with ivory and mother-of-pearl, were scattered about, on which were caskets filled with beautiful jewels and rare curios from foreign lands.

"The Princess herself was reclining on one of the cushions, sobbing as though her heart would break, and her beautiful hair was lying in dishevelled glory about her shoulders.

"I was afraid of alarming her, so I coughed slightly to attract her attention.

"She started up immediately with a look of terror, but was calmed in an instant when she saw who it was.

"'Oh!' she cried, 'have you slain him? You must have done in order to have reached here. Oh! have you come to save me?' and she looked at me with wild, eager eyes.

"'Calm yourself, fair lady!' said I. 'What is it that alarms you? Be sure that I will do all in my power to protect you from any evil that threatens you.'

"'The Dragon!' gasped the Princess. 'Have you not slain him? How else can you have entered? He lies at the door of the cave.'

"She caught me by the hand and led me to the entrance, and then, clasping one hand over her eyes and shuddering with terror, she pointed to where, a short distance beyond, under the shadow of some rocks, lay a terrible Dragon, watching with cruel and expectant eyes for any prey that might come his way.

"'I cannot get away from here except I pass him, and I have been imprisoned here now for two days,' sobbed the Princess. 'The King, my father, must indeed be distraught at my absence,' and she burst into fresh weeping.

"I pressed her to tell me how she came there, and she explained to me that one day, while walking on the sands with one of her maidens in attendance, they had together discovered this cave, which was only accessible at low tide; and they had secretly brought the rugs and tapestries and other furniture with which the cave was filled and made a bower of it, to which the Princess was wont to retire whenever she wished to be alone.

"And, venturing here two days since without attendance, the Princess had found, when she had wished to depart, the terrible monster lying in her path.

"'And so,' she cried, 'I have been a prisoner all this time.'

"I cheered her as well as I was able, and turned to my little book to see if by chance it gave me any directions how I might slay a Dragon by means of my fairy powers; and I read there that though one might not slay it (for a Dragon lives for a thousand years), one might rob it of its power by casting at it a jewel of great brilliancy, at the same time wishing that he might become dazed and impotent till one could escape, and it would be so.

"I told this to the Princess, and she hastened to unfasten from her bosom a jewel of great value set in gold of curious workmanship, which she gave to me, imploring me at the same time to do immediately as the book directed.

"'Nay,' said I, 'the jewel is yours; you must cast it at the Dragon, and I will *wish* that the fairies may aid us.'

"And so we stood at the door of the cave, and the Dragon, seeing us, came forward with wide-opened jaws.

"The Princess clung to my arm with one hand, but with the other she cast the jewel, while with all my desire I wished that my fairy powers might not fail me now.

"Whether, however, it was that the fairies willed it so, or perchance because she was a girl, the Princess's aim was not straight, and she hit, not the Dragon, but a great boulder in the shadow of which he was lurking; and then a truly remarkable thing occurred, for the boulder, immediately it was struck by the jewel, tumbled forward, and falling upon one beside it, imprisoned the Dragon between the two, where he has remained to this day."

And Shin Shira pointed dramatically to the rocks, from which an extra large puff of spray belched forth, with a groan and a cry which almost convinced me that what he told me must be true.

"And what became of the Princess after that?" I inquired, being anxious to hear the end of the story.

"Why," resumed Shin Shira, "we picked up the jewel and hurried away from the spot, and presently came at the top of the cliffs to the Castle, the ruins of which may still be seen up yonder—to where the King dwelt.

"I cannot tell you with what joy the Princess was received, nor with what honour and favour I was rewarded by the King—and, indeed, by all of the people—as the Princess's deliverer.

"It is enough to say that the King called a great assembly of people, and before them all said that as a fitting reward he should give me the fairest jewel in all his kingdom, and handed me the very stone which had been cast at the Dragon, and which was valuable beyond price, being one of the most perfect and flawless stones in the world.

"I was glad enough to have the gem, but I had fallen madly in love with the Princess's beauty, so I made bold to remind the King that the fairest jewel in his kingdom was not the gem he had given me, but the Princess, his daughter.

"The answer pleased the King and the people, though I remember sometimes sadly, even now, that the Princess's face fell as she heard the King declare that his word should be kept, and the fairest jewel of all, even the Princess herself, should be mine.

"But now, alas! comes the sorrowful part, for, before the ceremony of our marriage could be completed, I was doomed by the fairies to disappear, and so I lost for ever my beautiful bride," and Shin Shira gave a deep sigh. "The jewel though," he added, "remained mine, and I have always worn it in the front of my turban in honour and memory of the lovely Princess. You may like to see it," and Shin Shira reached up to his head for the turban in which I had noticed the jewel sparkling only a moment before.

It was gone!

"Dear me! I'm disappearing again myself, I'm afraid," said Shin Shira, looking down at his legs, from which the feet had already vanished.

"Good-bye!" he had just time to call out, before he departed in a little yellow flicker.

"Hi! Hi!" I heard voices shouting, and looking up to the cliffs I saw some people waving frantically. "Come up quickly, or you'll be cut off," they shouted.

And I hurried along the sands, only just in time, for I had been so interested in Shin Shira's story that I had not noticed how the tide had been creeping up. I shall have a good look at that jewel in Shin Shira's turban next time I see him—and as for "the Bellows," I hardly know which explanation to accept, Shin Shira's or that of the guide.

* * * * *

MYSTERY NO. III

THE MAGIC CARPET

It was just at the end of the school term, and I had received a letter from my young cousin Lionel, who was at Marlborough, reminding me of my promise that he should spend a part at least of his holidays with me.

"Mind you're at the station in time," he had said; "and, I say! please don't call me Lionel if there are any of our fellows about, it sounds so kiddish. Just call me Sutcliffe, and I'll call you sir—as you're so old—like we do the masters. Oh yes! and there's something I want you to buy for me, very particularly—it's for my study. I've got a study this term, and I share it with a fellow named Gammage. He's an awfully good egg!"

"What extraordinary language schoolboys do manage to get hold of," I thought as I re-read the letter while bowling along in the cab on my way to the station, which, a very few minutes later, came in sight, the platform being crowded with parents, relatives and friends waiting to meet the train by which so many Marlburians were travelling.

There was a shriek from an engine, and a rattle and clatter outside the station, as the train, every window filled with boys' excited faces, came dashing up to the platform.

"There's my people!" "There's Tom!" "Hi! hi! Here I am!" "There's the pater with the trap!" "Hooray!" To the accompaniment of a babel of cries like these, and amidst an excited scramble of half-wild school-boys, I at last discovered my small cousin.

"There he is!" he said, pointing me out to a young friend who was with him; and coming up he hurriedly offered his hand.

"How are you, *Sutcliffe*?" I asked, remembering his letter.

"All right, thanks," he replied. "This is Gammage. I wanted to show you to him. He wouldn't believe I had a cousin as old as you are. See, Gammage?"

Gammage looked at me and nodded. "'Bye, Sutcliffe; good-bye, sir," said he, raising his hat to me and hurrying off to his "people."

"I say! don't forget the rug, Sutcliffe!" he bawled over his shoulder before finally disappearing.

"Oh no! I say, sir! *That's* what I want to ask you about," said Sutcliffe, scrambling into the taxi, and settling himself down with a little nod of satisfaction.

"What?" I inquired, as we bowled out of the station.

"Why, a rug for my—our—study," said the boy. "Gammage has bought no end of things to make our room comfortable, and they've sent me up some pictures and chairs and things from home—and—it would be awfully decent of you if you'd buy me a rug to put in front of the fire-place. It's rather cheek to ask, but you generally give me something when I come over to see you, and I arranged with Gammage to say I'd rather have that than anything. What sort of a shop do you get rugs at? Couldn't we get it on our way now, and then it would be done with? I might forget to ask you about it later on."

"What sort of a rug do you want?" I asked, as the taxi turned into Tottenham Court Road.

"Oh, I don't know, sir. Any sort of an ordinary kind of rug will do. There's some in that window; one of those would do."

I stopped the taxi and we got out. The window was filled with Oriental rugs and carpets, and a card in their midst stated that they were "a recent consignment of genuine old goods direct from Arabia."

"Oh, they're too expensive, I expect," I remarked, as we stood amongst a small crowd of people in front of the window, "those Oriental rugs are generally so—"

But Sutcliffe suddenly nudged my arm, and, with an amused twinkle in his eye, called my attention to a remarkable little figure standing beside him, dressed in an extraordinary yellow costume, and wearing a turban.

"Why! bless me! It's Shin Shira!" I exclaimed. "I hadn't noticed you before."

"No," said the Yellow Dwarf, "I've only just appeared. How very strange meeting you here!"

I told him what we were doing, and introduced my young cousin, who was greatly interested and somewhat awe-struck at the extraordinary little personage in the Oriental costume, whose remarkable appearance was causing quite a sensation amongst the bystanders.

"Oh, these rugs," he said, looking at them casually. "No, I don't fancy they are much good for your purpose, they seem to be too—hullo!" he suddenly cried excitedly, "what's that? Good gracious! I really believe it's—Why, yes! I'm sure of it! I recognise it quite well by the pattern. There's not another in the world like it. How could it possibly have got here?"

"What *are* you talking about?" I asked.

"Why, this carpet," cried Shin Shira, pointing excitedly to a very quaint-looking Oriental rug in the corner of the window. "It's the Magic Carpet which everybody has read about in the *Arabian Nights*. It enables anybody in whose possession it is to travel anywhere they wish—surely you must have heard about it."

"No!" cried Lionel, his eyes sparkling with eagerness, "not really? Oh, sir! Do—*do* please buy it—it will be simply ripping! Do! do! Why, it will be better than an aeroplane."

I had never in my life before seen my cousin so excited about anything.

"I should certainly advise you to purchase it," whispered Shin Shira. "It is a very valuable rug, and no doubt you would find it very useful in many ways."

I must confess to a considerable amount of curiosity myself as we entered the shop and asked to be shown the carpet which Shin Shira declared to be endued with such remarkable properties.

It was a very handsome one, and the shopkeeper showed it to us with a considerable amount of pride.

"It's a genuine article, sir," he told me. "Came over only last week from Arabia in a special parcel purchased by our agent in Baghdad—I believe it's very old. These foreigners know how to make things which will last."

I inquired the price, and hesitated considerably when I found that it was far in excess of the amount I had intended to pay for a rug.

However, Lionel seemed so very eager, and Shin Shira assured me so positively that it was really a bargain, that, with a sigh at what I feared was a great piece of extravagance on my part, I took out my purse and paid for it. "To where shall I send it?" inquired the shopkeeper.

"Let's ride home on it and save the cab fare," whispered Shin Shira, pulling me down to his level by my sleeve.

"Good gracious!" I exclaimed.

"Why not? It will be the quickest way home, and certainly the least expensive," persuaded the little Yellow Dwarf.

"But—but—" I protested.

Shin Shira had already spread the carpet on the ground, and pulling Lionel on to it, beckoned me to follow.

Half mechanically I obeyed his instructions, and had no sooner sat down on it, cross-legged, as I saw that Shin Shira and Lionel were doing, than the little Yellow Dwarf cried out something in a language which I supposed to be

"We floated away over the roofs of the houses."

Arabic—and immediately we began to rise into the air.

I shall never forget the expression of dismay on the countenance of the shopkeeper and his assistants, when they saw us slowly floating in the air towards the door.

"Open it! open it, somebody!" shouted Shin Shira, and a bewildered-looking customer who had just entered instinctively pulled the handle. Before we knew where we were, we found ourselves out in the open air with a shouting, gesticulating, excited crowd watching us as we rose higher and higher, and floated away over the roofs of the houses.

The sensation, I must admit, was a pleasant one, and, despite a slight feeling of nervousness (which, however, young Sutcliffe did not appear to share), I quite enjoyed the journey to my flat.

There were, fortunately, but very few people about, and we arrived at the door without attracting much attention.

One nervous old lady, at whose feet we descended somewhat suddenly, did threaten to call the police—saying rather angrily that "What with motor-cars and such-like," she "didn't know what we were a-coming to, and it wasn't safe for a respectable lady to walk about the streets, what with one thing and another."

I managed, however, to soothe her ruffled feelings, and, rolling the rug up carefully, we went up to the flat. I threw myself into a chair in the study, thoroughly tired out and not a little bewildered by the strange events of the morning.

Lionel, however, was full of excitement, and eager to be off again for a ride on the marvellous Magic Carpet.

"I say! you know! but it's the rippingest thing I've ever heard of. Why, we'll be able to go anywhere. Just think what an awful lot we'll save in railway fares and cabs and those sort of things. I suppose anybody can use it?" he inquired, turning to Shin Shira.

"Oh yes, of course," declared the little Yellow Dwarf, "so long as you say, out loud, where you want to go to."

"Oh! Do let's go out again—just for a little while," pleaded Lionel. "Can't we go to Gammage's? He lives over at Wimbledon. It's quite easy to get to, and it won't take long. We could be back to lunch, and I should *so* like him to see the Magic Carpet. Do come, sir."

"No," I replied, shaking my head, "I'm too tired. You two can go if you like, only be back in an hour and a half."

"Oh, jolly!" cried Lionel. "Come on, please—let's start at once."

And he picked up the carpet under his arm.

"I think it would attract less attention if, instead of starting from the pavement, we went out of the window," said Shin Shira. "What do you say?"

"By all means," I replied, "if you think best," for you see, having ridden on it myself, I felt perfectly safe in trusting my young cousin on the Magic Carpet, and I felt sure that Shin Shira would not let him come to any harm.

So we opened the window, and a minute later the two were gaily floating away out of sight, both energetically waving their pocket-handkerchiefs until they disappeared.

I could tell by the noise in the street that their strange method of conveyance was attracting considerable attention; but as I felt thankful to note, no one seemed to connect their appearance with my rooms.

The next hour or so passed quickly enough, and I did not begin to get in the least anxious till I heard the clock strike two, and then I suddenly realised that they were over half-an-hour late.

"Oh, they're all right," I consoled myself with thinking. "I expect Gammage is so interested in the wonderful carpet that they can't get away."

When three hours had passed, however, and there was no sign of their return, I began to get seriously alarmed.

"What can have happened?" I thought, and, to add to my discomfiture, a telegram arrived from Lionel's parents inquiring if he had arrived in London safely from Marlborough.

I was able to reply, truthfully, that he *had* arrived safely, but, as hour after hour passed by without any trace of either Shin Shira or the boy, I became more and more disturbed.

At last I could stand it no longer, but putting on my hat, I hurried off to the nearest Police Station.

"H'm! What do you say, sir?" said the Police Inspector whom I found there, seated before a large open book, when in a broken voice I had hurriedly explained that I feared that my young cousin was lost. "Went off in company with a foreign-looking gent—Just describe him to me, please, as near as you can."

I described Shin Shira's appearance as accurately as I could, and the Police Inspector looked up hurriedly and gave me a searching glance.

"Do you mean to say the gent was going about the streets dressed like *that?*" he asked, when I had told him about Shin Shira's yellow costume and turban.

"Yes," I replied in some confusion, "he is a foreigner, you know, and—"

"Where does he come from?"

"From Japan, I think, or China, or—"

"What's his name?"

"Shin Shira Scaramanga Manousa Yama Hama is his full name, but—"

The Police Inspector laid down his pen and stared again at me.

"It's a curious name," said he; "I'll get you to write it down for me. I don't think I should be surprised at *anything* happening to *anyone* with a name like that. Where do you say they were going?"

"Well," I explained, "they set out to go to Wimbledon to see a—"

"Wimbledon? Let's see, from Kensington they'd go by train I suppose, from High Street Station, and change at—"

"No, no," I interrupted, "they didn't go by train at all, they—" and here I paused, for I suddenly reflected how exceedingly unlikely the Inspector would be to believe me if I told him exactly *how* they set out for Wimbledon. "You see," I began by way of explanation, "I bought a rug this morning that—"

"Excuse me, sir," said the Inspector somewhat impatiently, "would you mind keeping to the subject. How did Mr. Shin—er—the foreigner I mean, and your cousin go to Wimbledon? If they didn't go by train, did they drive or go by motor, or what?"

"Well, I was trying to tell you. You see, I bought a rug this morning, that—"

"I *don't* want to hear about your rug, sir," said the Inspector quite angrily. "If you wish us to try and find the young gentleman you must answer my questions properly. How did he set out to go to Wimbledon? Come, come! Let's begin at the beginning. Which way did they turn when they left your door?"

"You see, they didn't exactly leave by the door," I began.

"How did they go then, out of the window?" asked the Inspector in a somewhat sarcastic voice.

"Yes," I replied, "that's just how they did go."

The Inspector looked bewildered.

"Look here, sir," he said at last, "you told me when you gave me your name and address that you lived in a flat at Kensington on the second floor, and now you tell me that your cousin and a foreign gentleman with an outlandish name and dressed like a Guy Fawkes, left your house by the window. Really!"

"So they *did*," I explained; "you see, I bought a rug this morning that—"

"*Bother* the rug, sir!" shouted the Inspector, angrily throwing down his pen.

"If you *won't* listen to what I have to say," I said with some amount of dignity, "how can I possibly tell you what I know? I am *endeavouring* to explain that my cousin and the gentleman left in a very remarkable manner by means of a Magic Carpet, which—"

"Excuse me, sir," said the Inspector, getting up from his seat and showing me the door, "it strikes me that it's a lunatic asylum you want and not a Police Station. I haven't any time to waste with people who come here with stories like that. Good-evening!" And he shut the door, leaving me outside on the step.

I went to several other stations, and finally to Scotland Yard, but I could get no one to believe my extraordinary story; and at last I went to bed quite bewildered and in a terribly anxious frame of mind, leaving the lights burning and the windows wide open in case the wanderers returned during the night.

The next day, not hearing any news, I was obliged to telegraph for Lionel's father and mother; and I had a terrible scene with them, for they reproached me over and over again for letting their son venture out upon the Magic Carpet.

"You must have known," said my aunt tearfully, "that it was dangerous to trust to such heathenish and out-of-date methods of travelling, and now the poor dear boy is probably transformed or bewitched, or done something terrible to by this wretched Yellow Dwarf friend of yours, with the awful name. It's really disgraceful of you to have let him go at all!"

And so, amid the most bitter reproaches, although I left no stone unturned in my hopeless search for Lionel and Shin Shira, several days flew by, till one morning I nearly leaped from my chair in surprise and delight, at seeing the following report in the paper—

"EXTRAORDINARY RESCUE AT SEA

"By Marconigram comes a message from mid-ocean that two days ago the S.S. *Ruby*, from Liverpool to New York, picked up at sea, under extraordinary circumstances, an English school-boy who states that he was travelling by means of a Magic Carpet, which he was unable to manage. He was found to be in a state of complete exhaustion, but has since recovered, and appears to be a lively, intelligent lad. He will be landed at New York."

It is needless to say that my uncle and myself lost no time in putting ourselves in communication with the steamship people, and of course found that the rescued lad was no other than Lionel.

His father and I crossed over by the next boat, and found him happy and well and being made a tremendous fuss of by everybody at the hotel where we had arranged for him to stay till our arrival.

"Of course," he explained in telling us all about it, "everything went all right at first, and we went to Gammage's house in no time, but he was out. We landed in the garden, and nobody saw us, and I went up to the front door and knocked, and when I found Gammage wasn't at home I just went back to Shin Shira and asked where else we could go, because I didn't want to go home so soon.

"'How would you like to go over to France?' he said; 'we could do it in about twenty minutes.'

"So of course I said yes, and we were crossing the Channel all right when he suddenly began to disappear.

"You can guess I was in an awful funk when I found myself alone on the beastly old carpet, and I couldn't manage it at all. I suppose it was because I couldn't speak the language; Shin Shira used Arabic or something, wasn't it? I tried all sorts of things too, a little bit of French—you know, 'Avez-vous la plume de ma sœur?' and 'Donnez-moi du pain,' and things like that out of my French exercises, but it didn't do any good: we only went out to sea.

"It was frightfully cold all night, and I couldn't sleep at all, and I began to get awfully hungry; but the next morning about eleven o'clock I began to descend very slowly and gradually down to the sea. I thought I was going to be drowned, but fortunately just before I touched the water they saw me from the *Ruby*, and sent a boat out to pick me up. Everybody was awfully decent on board, and I had plenty of grub and changed my clothes. A fellow who was going over with his people lent me his while mine were being dried.

"Then when I got to New York your cable message was there waiting for me, so I knew it was all right."

We were very thankful to have found the boy again, and within three weeks we were happily home once more, and the adventure with the Magic Carpet was a thing of the past.

The carpet itself was left floating out at sea, and from that day to this I have not heard of it again.

* * * * *

MYSTERY NO. IV

SHIN SHIRA AND THE DUCHESS

It all began with the collar-stud—at least I put it down at that.

You see, I was dressing rather nervously to go to a charity "At Home" at the Duchess of Kingslake's. I had not met the lady previously, but some young friends of mine had been invited to the "At Home," and they had persuaded the Duchess to ask me too.

I do not know many titled people, and had never before visited a real live Duchess, so I was just telling myself that I must really be on my very best behaviour, and above all, that I must not be late in arriving. The card had mentioned "4 to 6.30," and it was past three o'clock now.

I was just struggling to fix my collar, which was rather stiff and tight, when suddenly the stud popped out and rolled away to—where?

Down I got on my hands and knees, and groped about in every direction that I could think of. I lit a candle, and searched in every available hiding-place; but no—no collar-stud could be anywhere found.

And the time was going on. I rang the bell for Mrs. Putchy, my housekeeper.

"Please, Mrs. Putchy, send at once to the nearest hosier's and buy me a plain collar-stud, and kindly ask Mary to get back as quickly as possible. I am expecting the cab every moment."

"It is at the door, sir," said Mrs. Putchy; "and I don't know, I'm sure, where Mary will be able to get a collar-stud for you to-day. This is Thursday, you know, sir, early closing day."

Too true. It was indeed *most* unfortunate. In my neighbourhood all the shops close at two o'clock Thursdays, and it would have been as easy to buy a collar-stud as an elephant at Kensington just then.

What was to be done?

A sudden inspiration struck me.

I ran across to the study, and undoing my desk, I found a little yellow-covered book attached to a golden chain which I had picked up just after my friend Shin Shira had vanished the last time he had visited me.

It was the book which the fairies had given him, and contained directions as to what to do when in any difficulty. I hurriedly turned to the letter C, intending to look for "collar-stud"—but, to my great disappointment, there was no such word to be found.

"Of course not," I suddenly thought; "the people who live in the land from which Shin Shira comes don't wear such things," and I let my mind wander back to my little friend with his yellow silk costume and turban.

"Hullo! though," I exclaimed a moment later, "what's this?"

My eyes had caught the words "*To obtain your wishes*" at the top of one of the pages.

I hastily read what followed, and gathered from what was written that *anybody* could have at least *two* wishes granted by the fairies if he only went about it in the right way and followed the given directions closely. It appeared that one must hop round three times, first on one foot and then on the other, repeating the following words aloud, and wishing very hard—

> "Fairies! fairies! grant my wishes,
>   You can do so if you will,
> Birds and beasts and little fishes
>   One and all obey you still.
> Fairies! Please to show me how
>   You can grant my wishes *now*."

Of course *I* immediately wished for a collar-stud, and I was just hopping round on my right leg for the third time, having begun with the left one, when Mrs. Putchy entered the room.

She looked rather surprised at seeing me engaged in what must have seemed to her rather an extraordinary occupation, but she is so used to strange things happening with me that she made no remark, except to point to a spot just in front of the fire-place, where, to my great surprise, I could see the very collar-stud which I had wanted.

"Extraordinary!" I exclaimed, as I picked it up. "I could have declared that it was not there a minute ago, for as you know, Mrs. Putchy, I searched everywhere for it."

"The cabman, sir, is getting impatient," said Mrs. Putchy, as she put down my coat and hat which she had thoughtfully brought to my room.

"Well, we won't keep him waiting long now," I smilingly said as I hurriedly completed my dressing, and a very few minutes later, the cab was quickly bowling me towards my destination.

The mansion near Grosvenor Square, at which the Duchess resided, was a very grand one, and red carpet was laid down the steps and across the pavement for the convenience of the guests, who were arriving in large numbers at the same time as myself. Fortunately, just inside the hall I met my little friends the Verrinder children; Vera, the little girl, looking very pretty in her white party frock; and her two brothers, Dick and Fidge, full of excitement and high spirits.

They fastened on me at once and dragged me most unceremoniously up to our hostess, who it appears was Vera's godmother, and introduced me in their own fashion.

"This is the gentleman who tells stories, godmamma," said Vera.

"And knows all about the Wallypug and the Dodo and Shin Shira, and all sorts of things," declared Dick.

"And if you ask him—" began Fidge, when the Duchess interrupted him.

"Really, children, you mustn't rattle on so. I am very pleased to meet your friend, and I trust that he will have an enjoyable afternoon," and the lady smiled graciously and held out the tips of her fingers for me to shake.

I bowed as politely as I knew how, and, following the children, was soon in the large drawing-room, which was already half filled with young people who had come to the "At Home."

It appeared that a very grand personage indeed was to be present. A real live Princess was coming to receive purses of money which the children had collected themselves, on behalf of the poor and sick in the East-end of London; and, after the purses had been given, there was to be a kind of concert and entertainment.

Footmen were walking about with tea and cakes of all sorts, and the time passed very pleasantly, till presently there was a commotion at the door, and Her Royal Highness the Princess entered and was led to the end of the room, where a tiny little girl presented a beautiful bouquet of flowers.

The Princess made a gracious little speech, saying how glad she was to come on behalf of the poor people to receive the purses of money which the children had collected; and then as they passed up one by one and laid their purses on the silver tray beside her, she had a smile and a little happy nod for each of them.

It was a very pretty sight, but soon over, for the Princess, who is devoted to good works, had to hurry away to another work of charity in a distant part of London.

We were all sorry when she went, but were not allowed to get dull, for almost immediately afterwards the concert began.

Several ladies and gentlemen sang, and a wonderful boy-pianist played some music of his own composing; a little girl played the violin delightfully; and a very humorous gentleman was giving a musical sketch at the piano and making us all laugh very much, when I suddenly noticed that the Duchess, who was sitting by herself on a settee, had raised her lorgnette and was staring curiously, and rather apprehensively, at something beside her.

It was yellow in colour and seemed to grow larger every minute. I had imagined at first that it was a cushion, but now it suddenly occurred to me that it was Shin Shira appearing.

Of course! and a minute or two later there he sat, cross-legged, composedly fanning himself on the settee beside the Duchess.

I could see her draw her skirts aside and regard the little Yellow Dwarf in a puzzled and bewildered manner; and, as soon as the musical sketch was concluded, she called one of the footmen to her and told him to "remove that extraordinary-looking person immediately."

Vera and the boys, however, had caught sight of Shin Shira, and flew forward to claim acquaintance with him.

"It's Shin Shira, you know, godmamma. He's a friend of the gentleman who came with us—and—"

"He was not invited," said the Duchess, looking with great disfavour at the little Yellow Dwarf, "and it was exceedingly impertinent of your friend to bring him without an invitation—I am displeased."

"Madam," said Shin Shira, getting down to the floor and bowing low in the Oriental manner, "you are mistaken in thinking that I came with a friend. I—er—appeared, because I was *obliged* to do so—I—"

The Duchess came over to where I was sitting.

"*Do* you know this person?" she inquired, pointing with her glasses towards Shin Shira. "Who and what is he? Did you bring him here, and if so why?"

"I am acquainted with the gentleman, Duchess," I admitted, "but he did not come with me. I can tell you, however, that now he is here he can be made very useful in entertaining your guests—he is a conjurer of very remarkable powers, and I've no doubt whatever but that he would be only too happy to exercise them for the amusement of the company."

"That is a different matter," said the Duchess, evidently somewhat mollified. "You may introduce me."

I went to fetch Shin Shira, and had soon performed the necessary ceremony.

"The Duchess would be very much obliged if you would perform some conjuring tricks, as I know you will do with pleasure," I whispered.

"Delighted, I'm sure," replied the little Yellow Dwarf; "that is one thing which I flatter myself I can do very well, owing to my fairy powers," and so it was arranged that he was to begin immediately.

I cannot possibly tell you of all the wonderful things he showed us. He made flowers grow straight up from the carpet, and turned a gentleman's walking-stick into a kind of Christmas-tree, upon which hung a little present for every child in the room: a fan for each of the ladies, and a suitable gift for each of the gentlemen.

This was a most popular trick, it is needless to say, and the numerous ladies and gentlemen who had by this time joined the party were as delighted as were the children themselves.

Shin Shira had become quite a centre of attraction, and the Duchess smiled at me approvingly.

"Your friend is a great acquisition," she remarked, coming over to the settee on which I was seated. "Look! look! whatever is he going to do now?"

I was as interested and puzzled as herself, for, knowing of the extraordinary powers which my

"Shin Shira placed them in the Crystal Bowl."

little friend possessed, I could never be sure what to expect from him in the way of the marvellous.

This time it was really a most interesting trick.

First of all he turned an inkstand into a large clear crystal bowl, and placed it on a little table which stood in front of him. Then he asked for anything to be given to him which the owner wished to disappear.

Several gentlemen gave their watches, and one or two ladies laughingly took off their bracelets and handed them to Shin Shira, who immediately placed them in the crystal bowl.

To our utter astonishment, each article as it was placed into the bowl vanished from sight, and Shin Shira turned the bowl upside down to show that nothing was inside.

"It's really most marvellous," murmured the Duchess, taking off a most valuable diamond ornament and handing it to the Yellow Dwarf. "Please make this disappear too. I shall value it more highly than ever if I know that it has been through such a wonderful adventure."

Shin Shira bowed, and taking the jewelled ornament from the lady, he dropped it into the bowl, where it at once shared the same fate as the other articles.

"Ha! Hum!" said a grave and somewhat pompous voice, "our friend here might readily become a very dangerous person if he exercised his remarkable gifts in private, and made things disappear in this extraordinary fashion, and then refused to produce them again. Eh? Ha! Hum!"

"Yes—ha! ha! very good. Ha! ha!" laughed a number of people who were standing near to the guest who had spoken.

"That's the Lord Chief Justice," explained a gentleman who stood near me. "That's why everybody is laughing; it's considered very improper not to laugh when the Lord Chief Justice makes a joke—however feeble it is."

I hardly listened to what he was saying, though, for I had suddenly noticed something which caused me a good deal of anxiety.

Shin Shira was beginning to look very thin and vapoury about the head, and, while I was watching him, to my horror, he began to vanish piecemeal till he had entirely disappeared from sight, after giving me a strange, apologetic look.

The people clapped and stamped and laughed, evidently imagining that it was all part of the trick—but I—*I* knew differently, and scarcely dared realise what it all meant for me.

For a few minutes everybody waited patiently for him to appear again, and clapped and stamped in great good humour. Presently, however, they began to get rather tired and impatient, and, after we had waited for about twenty minutes, the delay began to get very awkward.

"Why doesn't he come back?" inquired the Duchess, in an impatient voice, coming over to where I was standing. "The delay is becoming very embarrassing."

I turned very red, I am afraid, for I hardly liked to explain that the probability was that he would *not* come back at all.

"Several of my guests are wanting to go early, and they must have their jewellery before they depart," she continued. "Can you not tell him to hurry up?"

"I—I—I—am—afraid n—not," I stammered.

"But you *must*," insisted the lady. "He's your friend, and you brought him here, and I shall look to you to—"

"Oh, Duchess! I'm sorry to interrupt your charming party, but will you please ask the clever little gentleman who made my diamond and ruby bracelet disappear if he would kindly return it, as I really must be going," said a lady, hurrying up. "And my emerald chain, dear Duchess." "And my gold and pearl locket," chimed in several other voices.

"Yes, you simply must fetch him back somehow," said the Duchess, clutching my arm nervously. "You see my guests are beginning to get alarmed. You must!—you must!"

"B-but I can't—it's impossible," I endeavoured to explain.

The Duchess grew pale. "Do you mean to say," she gasped, "that the man has *really* disappeared—and—and taken the things with him? It's too terrible—too dreadful! What *am* I to do? And all my guests! What will they think of me? Oh! *Do—do—*do something! I don't mind so much about my beautiful diamond pendant, but do somehow get back the things belonging to my guests. You brought him here. You *must!*"

The grown-up guests were whispering together in little anxious and indignant groups, and things were beginning to look very serious—so serious that I sank into a chair and buried my head in my hands, trying to think of some possible way out of the difficulty.

The Duchess was almost in tears, and several ladies were trying to console her, when suddenly I thought of a means of escape. Of course! the wish! I had another wish left according to what the little book had told me. I had *wished* for a collar-stud, and had found my own. *Perhaps* if I wished for the jewellery—

The thought no sooner entered my head than I jumped up and began hopping on one leg repeating—

> "Fairies, fairies! grant my wishes,
> You can do so if you will,
> Birds and beasts and—"

"Oh, he's mad, he's gone mad. Hold him, somebody!" cried the Duchess when she saw me hopping about in what must have appeared to her a *most* eccentric manner; but, though several gentlemen came up and caught hold of me, I managed to get round three times on one leg, and three times on the other, repeating the magic rhyme, and then I wished—*wished* as hard as ever I could—for the jewellery to be found, before I sank down exhausted with my struggle.

Then a most remarkable thing happened, for the gentleman who had been pointed out to me as the Lord Chief Justice, and who had apparently been more indignant than anyone else at the disappearance of the jewellery, suddenly began behaving in a very strange manner too, diving his hands first into one pocket and then into another and muttering—"Strange! remarkable! Most extraordinary!" and finally drawing out from every part of his clothing watches, chains, rings, bracelets and jewellery of all kinds, till *every* missing article, including the Duchess's diamond pendant, was restored to its proper owner.

There was a pause at first, and then everybody began to talk at once—laughing and protesting that "of course they all *knew* it was part of the trick, and they weren't *really* anxious at all," and so on, and I knew that the situation was saved.

Even the Duchess beamed and admitted that it was "really *quite* the most marvellous performance she had ever seen," and thanked me over and over again for having introduced such a remarkable conjurer to her party. The guests were all equally delighted, and amidst the laughter and chatter that followed, the Verrinder children and myself made good our escape, and I felt very thankful that the fairies' "wish" had got me out of what at one time bid fair to have been a very awkward predicament.

* * * * *

The Duchess called on me the next day to thank me again, and to ask where she might write to my little friend to thank him also. This information, however, I was naturally unable to impart.

* * * * *

MYSTERY NO. V

SHIN SHIRA AND THE LAME DUCK

It was during the summer holidays and my young cousin Lionel was staying with me again. We had been spending the hot afternoon strolling about Kensington Gardens, and had just been enjoying a cup of tea and some cakes under the trees at the little refreshment place near the Albert Memorial.

"I think we'd better be going home now," I said. "We'll get a motor-'bus at the gate."

"Oh! must we go yet?" pleaded Lionel. "It's so jolly out here under the trees. Let's walk home past the Round Pond."

"I've some letters to write before dinner," said I, "but—"

"Oh, bother the old letters!" interrupted Lionel. "It won't take much longer to walk, and you'll get them done all right. Come on!"

With a sigh of resignation, I not altogether unwillingly let the young scamp have his way.

It was the best part of the day: the lengthening shadows and the cool breeze which had sprung up made walking very enjoyable.

We had nearly reached the Round Pond when I heard a startled "squ-a-a-k!" at my feet, and a lame duck struggled up from the grass and limped painfully off.

"Poor thing!" cried Lionel, who was a kind-hearted little chap. "You nearly trod on it. I wonder how it got to be lame."

"Some boys," said an indistinct voice close at hand, "some boys threw a stone at it this afternoon and injured its leg."

We looked round in great surprise, for there seemed to be nobody about to account for the voice; but presently I could just discern Shin Shira's face and yellow turban appearing.

"Can't shake hands yet," said he, nodding amiably, "for they haven't arrived at present, but I've no doubt they'll be here shortly."

"I wonder how he'd get on if he wanted to scratch his nose," whispered Lionel, who had a keen sense of the ridiculous.

"It's rude to whisper in company," said Shin Shira severely, evidently aware that some remark had been made about himself—"but there, you're only a boy, and boys are—Hullo! here come my legs! that's all right! I thought I shouldn't have to wait long for them. Where are you off to?" and the little Yellow Dwarf hurried up to us now that he was quite complete.

"Oh, we're just walking home," I replied, "only Lionel had a fancy to pass the Round Pond on our way; the little model yachts one often sees there are very amusing to watch."

"Yes," agreed Shin Shira. "There's one been left behind to-day," he continued. "The boys who threw the stone at the duck were seen by the park keeper, and when he came after them they ran away, leaving their boat behind them. Serve them right if they lose it."

"Oh, yes! There it is now!" cried Lionel, running towards the edge of the Round Pond. "What a jolly little yacht. Why, it's a perfect model," and he regarded it with the greatest admiration. He took it from the water and inspected it carefully.

"I say!" he cried excitedly, "wouldn't it be ripping if we could become small enough to go for a sail in it!"

"It's a very simple matter to arrange, if you wish it," remarked Shin Shira composedly.

"D-do you really m-mean that it would be possible for you to make us as tiny as that?" stammered Lionel in his eagerness, his eyes bright with excitement.

"I couldn't do it, but the fairies might," said the Dwarf, taking up the little yellow book which I had restored to him after our last adventure.

"But should we be able to return to our proper size again?" I inquired carefully, for I remembered from previous experience that Shin Shira's magical powers had an unfortunate habit of going wrong at times.

"Without the least doubt," replied he; "in fact, from the time that you are reduced to the size which you desire to be, you very gradually increase, till your original size is reached."

"Then there's no danger?" I hazarded.

"None whatever," was the reassuring reply.

"Then do, *do* please let us be 'reduced,'" pleaded Lionel eagerly.

"Very well, then," said I. "And do you propose that we should go for a trip in the model yacht?"

"Of course!" declared Lionel.

"Put it in the water then," said Shin Shira, "and I'll see what I can do."

Lionel quickly put down the boat, and stood watching Shin Shira to see what would happen.

The little Yellow Dwarf was busily gathering pebbles from the edge of the pond, examining each carefully, and then throwing them down again in what appeared to be an aimless and unintelligible manner.

Presently, however, he said, "There's *one*," and putting a stone carefully away in his belt, he continued to search till he had found another like it.

"And there's the other," he said, coming towards us.

"Now then, all you have to do is to swallow these two little white stones and wish to be—let's see—an inch and a quarter high, and there you are."

"It seems rather a venturesome proceeding," I said, hesitatingly.

"Oh no! it'll be all right! Come along! Let's swallow them!" cried Lionel, suiting the action to the word and popping one of the stones into his mouth without further ado.

He immediately became so small that I had some difficulty in seeing him at all amongst the stones at the edge of the Pond.

"Are you not going to swallow one of the stones too?" I inquired of the Dwarf before swallowing mine.

"No, I think not," was the reply. "I'll remain as I am, I think, in case you may require assistance of a kind which only a larger person than yourself could afford."

I then swallowed my stone, and immediately became almost as tiny as my small cousin, having, for my part, wished to be reduced to the height of an inch and a half, thinking that *some* sort of distinction ought to be preserved in our relative sizes.

"There!" exclaimed Lionel in a vexed voice, when I had joined him. "It's no use after all! How on earth are we going to get on board?"

"Ah!" cried Shin Shira, laughing good-humouredly and now looking, to us, like a good-natured giant, towering as he did high above our heads. "*Now* you see the wisdom of my having remained as I am. I can simply lift you on board and push the boat off for you too."

Suiting the action to the word, he very gently and carefully picked up first Lionel and then me from the ground and placed us on board the yacht, then gave the boat a little shove which, though he didn't intend it to do so, sent us both sprawling on the deck and the boat itself well out into the water.

I think I have mentioned that a slight breeze had sprung up, and the Pond was rippled over with tiny waves, upon which our yacht danced merrily, the sails having filled out with wind which drove her along at a fine rate.

Lionel was running all over the deck examining everything eagerly.

"I wish there was a real cabin," he said; "this is only a dummy one, and I find a lot of the ropes to the sails won't act properly. I wonder how you steer the thing, too."

"By means of the rudder, I should imagine," I said.

"Of course!" exclaimed Lionel impatiently; "any baby would know that; but this one is fastened up so tightly that I can't move it."

"Well, never mind," said I, "it is evidently set in the right direction; for see, we are heading straight across the Pond, and there's Shin Shira walking round to be there to meet us when we go ashore," and I settled myself down comfortably to enjoy the pleasant trip.

"Hullo! Look at that!" cried Lionel a moment or two later, pointing to the shore.

The lame duck had been disturbed by Shin Shira's passing, and was slowly waddling towards the water.

"She's coming in!" declared Lionel. "By Jove! doesn't she look a size now we're so tiny!"

The boy was right, for, to us, the duck now appeared a formidable monster of strange and uncouth shape. Her bill, as she came quacking into the water, opened and shut in an alarming manner, revealing the fact that, if she desired to do so, she could make a meal of us at one gulp.

Somewhat to our dismay, she seemed impelled by some vague curiosity to swim in our direction, and the situation began to get distinctly alarming as she drew nearer and nearer.

"What on earth shall we do?" exclaimed Lionel. "I hope to goodness she isn't going to attack us. It would be too silly to be swallowed by a duck."

"I fancy she's only coming to have a look at us," I said, "and at any rate, if we shouted at her loudly if she came too near it would probably frighten her away."

This seemed to be the only thing to do, and as the duck continued to swim directly towards us we both began to shout and wave our arms about in what must have appeared to Shin Shira a perfectly mad fashion.

The noise, however, seemed to have the desired effect, for the duck paused, looked at us in a puzzled manner for a moment, and then turned tail and began moistening her bill in the water, lifting her head and shaking it after each mouthful, as their habit is.

"I wish she'd get out of the way," said Lionel anxiously. "We shall run into her directly, she's right in our course," and he began to shout vigorously again, in the hope of startling her.

I added my voice to his, and we both yelled our loudest, with not the slightest effect, however, for the duck continued unconcernedly to enjoy herself in her own fashion in the middle of the lake. Presently what Lionel had feared came to pass, and with a bump which sent us both off our feet, the yacht was driven straight on to the duck, which gave a terrific "Quack!" and swam off in a hurry.

"Our bowsprit's broken," announced Lionel, directly he had recovered his feet, "and it's fallen in the water and is dragging the sails with it—and—look out!" This as a gust of wind filled the mainsail and caused the boat to careen over on to her side in a highly dangerous manner.

"Look out!" and this time another and a stronger gust completed the matter, and the sail touched the water and immediately became saturated, so that the boat could not right itself.

"Well, we shan't sink, that's one thing," I said, for Lionel was looking at me in an alarmed manner. "The water cannot get into the hull, thanks to there not being a 'real' cabin and the hatches only being sham ones."

"That's all very well," said Lionel, though giving a little sigh of relief at my reassuring words, "but we can't stop here for ever. I should like to know how we are to get ashore."

Shin Shira, who had seen our accident, was shouting and gesticulating at the edge of the Pond, but the wind was blowing in his direction and carried the sound of his voice away from us, so that we couldn't hear a single word of what he was saying.

"I suppose eventually we shall drift ashore," I said hopefully.

"Yes, but not for hours and hours perhaps," said Lionel dolefully, "because the wind may change, you know, and besides it's getting dusk."

"It certainly isn't a very pleasant look-out," I agreed. "I can't see what we are to do, unless—I say! what's that big box floating towards us?"

Lionel looked in the direction in which I was pointing.

"It's an empty match-box," he said uninterestedly; "that's no good."

"I'm not so sure about that," said I. "Try and get hold of it as it drifts this way. I've an idea."

"I can't see what good an empty match-box can be to us," grumbled Lionel, doing his best, however, to aid me in capturing the prize as it blew against the side of the overturned yacht, which we at last did with some difficulty.

It was a very large box and had evidently been in the water for some time; the paper around it had become unstuck from the sides and hung loose in the water beside it.

"We must get the paper at all cost, and pray be careful not to tear it," I cried.

"Whatever for?" asked Lionel in amazement.

"Do as you're told and don't ask questions," I replied rather crossly, for I was very anxious to try an experiment which I had in my mind. So we hauled the paper aboard and stretched it on the bulwarks to dry.

Then we hauled the broken bowsprit aboard and freed it from the broken ropes with our pen-knives—a long and difficult job— and by the time we had finished, the paper which had been around the box had become dry and quite stiff by reason of the gum with which it had been stuck to the sides of the box.

"Oh, I see!" cried Lionel, as I clambered on to the box (which was fastened by a rope to the side of the yacht) and began to cut a hole in the middle. "You're going to make a raft."

"I'm going to try to," I answered grimly, for I wasn't at all sure that my experiment would be a success.

By dint of real hard work, cutting and contriving, however, we did eventually succeed in making a raft of a sort, the stiff paper, fixed to the broken bowsprit, making a capital sail; and somewhat in fear and trembling, we both got aboard and pushed off from the derelict yacht.

All went well for some time till we were nearing the shore, and then I noticed something which caused me grave alarm.

We were both growing rapidly! The raft, which had before been quite large enough to support us, was now low down in the water with our weight, and there was great danger of the water getting into the inside of the box, in which case it would undoubtedly sink.

Lionel noticed the difficulty at the same time as myself, for he gave me a startled glance.

"We're getting bigger," he said. "Do you think the raft will hold out?"

"I don't think so," I replied, "but we're quite near the water's edge now—perhaps I could swim ashore with you."

"Good gracious! I can swim twice that distance myself, thank you. Why, I beat Mullings Major hollow in the swimming competition last term, and he's four years older than me, and—"

Whatever Lionel was going to add was lost, for at that instant he had to put his boasted prowess to the test. The box, having filled with water just as I had feared it would do, sank slowly down, and we were left in the water.

Fortunately Lionel's boast was not a vain one, and he reached the shore before I did, laughing and wringing the water out of his clothes.

"Well, it's good to be on dry land once more at any rate," he said, as I waded ashore, "isn't it?"

"Yes," I agreed, looking about to see if I could discover any traces of Shin Shira in the dusk.

"There he is!" at last cried Lionel, "but his head has vanished, and there are only his legs and arms waving about. *They* won't be much use to us, and—by Jove! yes! Look, here comes that wretched old duck after us. We'll have to cut," and he gathered up his things and set the example.

It was quite true; the old duck had evidently come to the conclusion that we were something dainty to eat—in the frog line probably—and was waddling towards us as quickly as her game leg would allow.

Fortunately we were soon able to out-distance her; and having fixed our latitude by Kensington Palace, which we could just see in the distance, we set out for the gate.

To our tiny, but rapidly growing bodies the distance seemed an interminable one, especially as darkness was now quickly falling. We could see the lights in Kensington, but they seemed far, far away; and to add to our dismay, when at last, tired and exhausted, we did reach the gate, it was only to find it closed for the night, and that during our journey from the Pond we had grown too big to be able to squeeze through the railings.

We waited a few minutes uncertain what to do, till presently a cab came in sight, the horse walking leisurely and the cabby evidently on the look-out for a fare.

"Cabby! cabby!" I called, and Lionel added his shrill voice to mine.

The cabman looked about in bewilderment.

"Here, by the Park gates!" I yelled, and he got down from his seat and came over to where we were standing.

"Well, I'm blowed!" he exclaimed when he had had a good look at us. "What the Dickens are you? Kids or dwarfs or what?"

"Never mind what we are, cabby; get us out of here somehow, and drive us home to Kensington Square, and I'll give you a sovereign."

"Will you, though?" said the cabby. "Well, I'm gaun to do it, but the question is—how? I'll go and knock up the park keeper."

"No, no, don't do that!" I said hastily. "He'll want such a lot of explanations, and we're wet and uncomfortable and anxious to get home. Do please try and think of some way of getting us out without having to call him."

Our cabby was a man of resource, for having considered for a moment, he backed the horse close against the gate, stood on the top and lowered the horse's nosebag by means of a long rope which he kept by him in case of emergencies, and cried—

"Now then, get in there, one at a time, and I'll soon have you over here."

Lionel got in first, and as the cabby had said, was easily hauled up and deposited on the top of the cab.

I followed, and in a very short space of time we were both inside the cab and rattling home at a good pace.

I got the cabby to knock at the door, and Mrs. Putchy, to whom I quickly explained everything, gave him a sovereign for me. In a very few minutes Lionel and I were warm and comfortable each in our respective beds.

In the morning we had both grown to our original sizes, and the adventure of the day before was nothing but a memory.

* * * * *

MYSTERY NO. VI

SHIN SHIRA AND THE DIAMOND

I was exceedingly surprised a few weeks after our latest adventure with the little Yellow Dwarf to receive the following extraordinary letter from him. It was dated from Baghdad, and bore two very unusual postage stamps, which Lionel promptly claimed for his collection.

> "Kind and obliging Sir," it began, "I am in great and serious trouble and in danger of my life, and I appeal to you to come to my assistance by the first boat. I will explain everything when we meet, but kindly do not delay, as everything depends upon your presence here.
> "Again beseeching you not to delay,
> "Your miserable and much-afflicted friend,
>
> "SHIN SHIRA SCARAMANGA MANOUSA
> YAMA HAWA.

"P.S.—Inquire for me at the State Prison, Baghdad."

"Well!" I exclaimed, after perusing this remarkable epistle, "of all the extraordinary requests I have ever received this is the strangest. This man, whom I have only met at the most half-a-dozen times in my life, expects me to neglect my work and rush off to Baghdad, of all places in the world, to his assistance, because he has got into some trouble which has landed him in the State Prison there. I always thought somehow that those uncanny powers which he possesses would get him into serious difficulties at some time or another. I'll send him a letter stating that I cannot go to him." And here I endeavoured to dismiss Shin Shira and his affairs from my mind.

I was so worried about the matter, however, that I couldn't settle to work, so I lit my pipe and settled myself in my easy-chair to think the matter out.

Poor little fellow! If he really was in such desperate straits it seemed very heartless to leave him to his fate if in any way I could be of real assistance to him; and, after all, I could work almost as well while I was away as I could at home, and the voyage would probably give me plenty of new ideas for my book. I thought of all the kind things the little chap had done for me, and how he had always somehow come to the rescue when I had been in difficulties in my adventures with him; and finally I came to the conclusion that it would be most ungrateful and selfish of me if I let anything stand in the way of my going to my friend's assistance.

I had no sooner made up my mind on this point than I called a cab and set out at once for Messrs. Cook's office and booked a passage by the next steamer.

I will not tell you anything about the somewhat uninteresting journey either by sea or land, with the exception that when I at last stepped ashore in an Oriental port, I found in the curious costumes and strange surroundings many things to amuse me and to wonder at.

The entire journey on the whole, however, was decidedly tedious, and I was very glad to find myself at last in the ancient city of Baghdad.

I went at once to the British Consul there and told him my object in coming to the city.

"Shin Shira!" he exclaimed. "Why, there is scarcely anything talked about in these days but Shin Shira. He has stolen one of the most valuable crown jewels, and was caught with it in his possession. Despite the indisputable evidence against him, however, he persists in declaring his innocence, and pleads that, with the assistance of a friend from London, he can prove it conclusively. I suppose, sir, that you are the friend from London."

I told him that I was, and that I was deeply grieved to hear of the trouble that Shin Shira was in, and that I felt convinced that there was some mistake in the matter which could somehow or other be cleared up.

"I should be very glad to think so," said the Consul, shaking his head, "but I fear it is hopeless. You see, the stone—an almost priceless diamond—was actually found in his possession. But come, you will be anxious to see your friend as soon as possible. I will come with you to the prison and see that you are admitted."

The kind-hearted official called his carriage, and together we drove through the unfamiliar narrow streets to the dismal-looking building in which my poor friend was confined.

A brief consultation with the authorities and the signing of various papers made me free to enter the prison, and having thanked the Consul for his kind offices, I was led away by one of the officials to a terribly dark dungeon, in which, crouched in a corner, I found my poor friend Shin Shira, looking the picture of misery.

His face lit up with a smile of hope, however, when he saw me, and his whole aspect changed.

"My friend! my deliverer!" he cried, using all kinds of extravagant Oriental phrases to express his delight at seeing me. "Ah! at last you have come, and I shall be saved! May all the blessings of Allah be on your head!"

The official withdrew, locking the door carefully behind him, having first given me to understand by various signs that he would return for me in about half-an-hour.

"Well, now," I inquired, when we were alone, "what is this terrible trouble which has brought you here? What have you been doing?"

"Nothing!" declared Shin Shira solemnly. "Nothing whatever to merit this punishment. It is all a horrible mistake. Let me begin at the beginning. About two months ago, after a series of my usual adventures, I suddenly appeared here in Baghdad. Now I have been acquainted with the city for many, many years—in fact, ever since the time of Sinbad the Sailor, whom I knew quite well, and with whom I was at one time very friendly. Well, I have many times appeared here since then, and on each occasion I have taken a great interest in the place on account of old associations. I have made many friends here, too; so when I found myself here once more I was greatly delighted, and was making my way to the Bazaar, where I knew I should be sure to find some acquaintances, when greatly to my surprise I saw several passers-by stop and stare at me curiously and then, whispering amongst themselves, follow me at some distance behind.

"It could not be my clothing which was attracting all this attention, for it was more or less of the same pattern to which they were accustomed. I caught sight of myself in a polished steel mirror in one of the shops in the Bazaar, and stole a glance at myself, but could see nothing wrong. What could be the cause? I had not long to wait, however, before I found out to my cost what was wrong.

"The crowd following me had increased in size, and at last two enormous men in uniform came up and seized me by my arms, and I was immediately surrounded by a throng of curious faces.

"'Where did you get that diamond?' demanded one of my captors, pointing to my turban, in which, as you know, I always wear the jewel which the Princess gave me.

"'Oh that! That was given to me many years ago by a friend—a Princess—who has been dead now for many hundreds of years,' I said.

"'Many hundreds of years? And you say she was a friend of yours?' exclaimed the man. 'Absurd!'

"'Preposterous!' declared the other. 'Look here! If you can't give us some more reasonable explanation than that, we shall take you off at once to the Chief Magistrate, and charge you with having stolen it.'

"'But why?' I gasped. 'Why should you think that I have stolen it?'

"'A diamond of exactly that size and colour has disappeared from amongst the Crown jewels, and it strikes me very forcibly that this is the very one.'

"It was in vain for me to protest. I was taken before the Magistrate, and experts were called to examine the jewel.

"They weighed it and examined it carefully through powerful magnifying glasses, and finally unanimously agreed that it was indeed the missing jewel.

"I was closely cross-questioned as to how it came into my possession, and also as to my movements during the past six months. My explanations were considered most unsatisfactory, and no one would believe me; consequently I was thrown into prison and condemned to death. It was only by the most earnest pleading that I managed to gain time for you to get here, as I assured them that you would be able to put everything right, and explain matters to their entire satisfaction."

"I?" I stammered. "I am very, very sorry for you, my poor friend, and I would do anything to help you, but what am I to say or do which will convince them when you tell me that you have failed to do so?"

"It is easy—easy," declared Shin Shira hopefully. "Now attend carefully to what I say. I am of course not allowed outside the prison walls, and there is no one here whom I would dare to trust with an important commission.

"Now I want you to go at once to the Bazaar, and find a man named Mustapha, a dealer in old curiosities; and, without letting him know whom it is for, purchase from him a large round crystal which you will find in his shop. He will probably want a lot of money for it, but whatever he asks offer him just half, and you will find that after a lot of argument he will let you have it at that. These Oriental shopkeepers are all like that. And then, having secured the crystal, hurry back here and the rest will be easy."

Although I could not in the least see what Shin Shira wanted the crystal for, I was careful to execute his commission to the letter.

I found no difficulty in reaching the Bazaar, and, once there, soon found out Mustapha. I did not like the look of the man at all.

He was a fawning, obsequious little man, with shifting eyes which never looked you straight in the face.

He stood bowing and smiling and rubbing his hands when I entered the shop and asked to see the crystal.

"Ah yea—very fine crystal—for those who know how to use it. Very vallyble—lot money. You know this? You got?" and he gave me a searching glance with his little bead-like eyes.

"Oh yes, I can pay for it if I want it," I said, "but what do you call a *lot* of money? How much do you want for it?"

He named a price which I knew to be very excessive, and I shook my head decidedly.

"No! too much!" I declared.

"Oh! but see! Beautiful crystal!" he argued.

"No," I replied, "too much! I'll give you half," and I began to walk unconcernedly out of the shop.

"And you give me little present besides?" pleaded Mustapha.

"Not a penny," said I.

The man gave a little sigh.

"Oh well, you take him," he said. "Not enough money, but Mustapha very poor, must sell him. I wrap him up for you, see!"

I paid him the money and hurried out of the shop, for I must confess that I had taken a great dislike to the little man with his smooth, oily manner.

However, I had got the crystal, and that was the main thing.

I hastened back to the prison, and after a long argument with the authorities, I managed to gain permission to see the prisoner once more.

I found Shin Shira all eagerness to know if I had secured the crystal, and when he saw it in my hand, his joy knew no bounds.

"Now it is all easy," said he, "and I shall soon be free. This is a Magic Crystal, and by wishing very hard to see any particular object and gazing at it steadily for a moment or two, you will see just what you wish to see reflected in it. Now I'm just going to wish to—er—to—er—er—o—o-h! I'm going to vanish! To think that I've been here all this time hoping every day that I should be able to disappear, and now, just as I was about to get myself free—I—good-bye—!"

And to my horror, the little Yellow Dwarf suddenly faded away, and I was left alone in the dungeon.

I say to my horror, for what was I to say when the jailer appeared? How was I to account for the prisoner's escape? I was just puzzling about these things when the door opened and the jailer hurriedly came to tell me the time allowed for my visit was up.

He saw at once that Shin Shira was not there, and in a great state of excitement plied me with questions.

I felt, however, that the best thing to do was to preserve silence: it would at least gain time; so I shook my head and pretended not to understand a word of what he was saying in his broken English.

The man doubly locked the door and hurried off to inform his superior officers, and I was left alone once more.

My eyes fell upon the crystal, and I suddenly thought of what Shin Shira had said. Holding it carefully in my hands, I wished to see the real thief who had stolen the crown jewel.

A vague mist spread over the crystal, which gradually cleared away, and I distinctly saw revealed the features of—Mustapha. Then I wished to see what he had done with the stone, and after gazing a moment or two longer, I saw him take it down to a cellar under his shop and bury it in a tin box under a stone, which he lifted up from the floor.

That was enough for me. When the jailer and the other officers came hurrying back I was ready for them.

"Where is the prisoner?" they demanded.

"He has escaped," I replied coolly.

"What!" they exclaimed. "You dare to admit this, and that you assisted him to do so? You shall take his place here, and will no doubt receive the punishment which was intended for him."

"He is an innocent man," said I calmly, "and ought never to have been imprisoned. He did not steal the diamond."

"How can you say that when we found it upon him? Why, he was actually impudent enough to go walking about in the street with it boldly stuck in his turban."

"The stone he was wearing was his own, and he had every right, to wear it where and how he liked," I replied steadily.

"His own! Pooh! a likely story. Where is the missing jewel then? Can you tell me that?"

"Yes," I replied, to their great astonishment.

"And the thief?" they questioned eagerly.

"I know who he is too. Take me before the Magistrate at once, and I will soon restore the lost jewel."

My assured tone of voice seemed somewhat to impress the officials, and they left me for a few moments to consult amongst themselves as to what was best to be done.

Presently they returned and told me to follow them.

I found myself conducted to a plainly-furnished room where a dignified-looking gentleman was seated at a table strewn with papers. He looked up at me sharply as we entered the room, and addressing me in excellent English, said—

"What is this extraordinary story I hear about the escape of the prisoner Shin Shira, and that you are prepared to inform us of another person who has, as you say, the crown jewel in his possession?"

"It is true," said I, "and if you will allow some of your officers to accompany me into the Bazaar I will point out the thief at once, and show you where he has hidden the stone."

The Magistrate thought for a moment. "I will come with you myself," he said at last. "Have ready six men to accompany us," he commanded; and a few minutes later we were on our way to Mustapha's shop.

The wretched man gave a start and turned very pale when he saw us, but endeavouring to put a bold face upon it, he came bowing and cringing towards us, smiling and wringing his hands.

"What an honour to my poor house!" he exclaimed. "How unworthy am I to receive such august guests!"

"We've come to see if you have any more crystals like the one I bought of you to-day, Mustapha," I said.

"Alas! honoured patron, none!" cried Mustapha in a relieved voice, thinking that he now knew the object of our visit.

"Think—think, Mustapha," said I. "Have you no piece of clear glass that could be used in its place?"

"I took up the stone"

"Alas, none!" he replied, shaking his head.

"Look about," said I. "Here in the shop—and down in the cellar."

The little man's face turned green.

"The cellar? Noble patron, how should I find such a thing there?"

"Lead the way and I will try to show you," said I; and despite his agonised protests, the trembling wretch was made to lead us to the very spot where the jewel was hidden.

I took up the stone and showed the Magistrate the box in which the diamond was concealed, while Mustapha grovelled on the ground, pleading for mercy.

What followed was a matter of course. The merchant Mustapha was arrested, I was released and commissioned to let Shin Shira know that if he applied in person for his jewel it would be returned to him, and an apology offered for his unwarranted arrest.

And so I was set free—a stranger and alone in Baghdad.

* * * * *

MYSTERY NO. VII

SHIN SHIRA AND THE ROC

When I found myself alone in Baghdad after my extraordinary adventure with the Magic Crystal, my first intention was to return at once to England.

I found, however, that it would be impossible for me to do so for at least four days; so I prepared to make the best of matters by doing a little sight-seeing while I was still confined to the ancient and interesting city.

There were two additional reasons which made the delay less disagreeable to me.

The first one was that I might possibly happen to meet Shin Shira again before I departed; and the other was that, on the second day of my stay, I saw a printed notice to the effect that, according to the ancient usage of the country relating to condemned prisoners, all of Mustapha's goods were to be immediately sold by public auction, and the money realised was to be confiscated by the Crown.

I had noticed a number of very quaint and curious articles in the shop, and thought that it would be an excellent opportunity for me to purchase some souvenirs of my visit, to take back with me to England.

The sale took place the next day, and I was able to secure several interesting pieces, which have a place in my study to this day. In fact, I was tempted to buy so many things that I began to fear that I should soon not have enough money left to take me back again to London; and I was just about to leave the auction, in order to be out of the way of temptation, when I caught sight of the quaintest, most uncanny-looking brass lamp being offered for sale that you could possibly imagine.

It was slightly damaged too, and looked very old, so I hoped that it might be going very cheap.

I was right, and to my great delight it was knocked down to me for a mere trifle.

Clutching my treasures about me, I hurried back to my hotel, and spent the whole of the rest of the day examining and admiring my purchases.

The lamp, though, pleased me most of all, although it was so old and battered. It was so very quaint and uncommon, and so typically Oriental in design—in fact, I felt sure there was not another like it in the world.

The time came, however, for packing up, and I had to get everything ready for the morning, so that I might be in time for the early train.

I had carefully wrapped up the other things, and was just taking a last look at the lamp before putting it into the bag, when, turning around for no apparent reason, I caught sight of a yellow turban on the floor.

"Dear me!" I thought, "I suppose I must have brought this away from the Bazaar, with my other things, by mistake. What a nuisance! Now I shall have to take it back again, I suppose, or— No! it's Shin Shira's. And here comes the rest of him!" for I could see a little hazy yellow figure gradually growing out of nothing.

"Ah! just in time, I see," said the little fellow, when he had quite appeared. "I did so hope that I should be able to be visible again before you left Baghdad. Well, how did you get on? You've got out of prison, I'm glad to see."

I told him about the crystal, and how I discovered that it was Mustapha who stole the diamond.

"Phew!" he whistled when he heard this. "I felt sure someone had stolen it, but I didn't think of Mustapha. I never liked the man, though, personally, and I'm glad he's found out at last. He has done a lot of harm to many people in Baghdad, and he will be rightly punished. What is to be done with *my* diamond?" he inquired anxiously.

"Oh, you're to have it back whenever you like to go for it, and you'll receive an apology at the same time," said I.

"Very well, then, I'm off to get it first thing in the morning," said the little fellow gleefully. "I prize that stone far above its intrinsic value, for it was given to me by my beautiful Princess, you know, and I would not lose it for anything. But, I say! what's that curious-looking old lamp in your hand? May I look at it?"

I handed it over to him.

"It's just a little thing which took my fancy at Mustapha's sale, and which I picked up for a trifle," said I.

"It's very dirty—wants cleaning badly," declared Shin Shira. "Why, I believe it's solid brass, though it looks like rusty iron in its present neglected state," and he seized a duster which was lying handy and gave the lamp several smart rubs.

"Just as I thought," said he, going on vigorously with the polishing. "Why, it's splendid—"

"Oh!" I exclaimed, sinking into a chair. "See! see what you've done!"

An enormous form was rising from the floor, and presently stood before us making a deep salaam.

"W-who are you?" I stammered.

"The Slave of the Lamp, Master," said he.

"Good gracious!" I exclaimed, "you don't mean to say that this is—"

"Aladdin's lamp," burst in Shin Shira. "I thought somehow that it looked familiar. I knew Aladdin well, and I've often handled this lamp before."

"Impossible!" I exclaimed, gazing at the big black giant who stood, with his arms folded, in dignified silence before us.

"Nothing is impossible in the East," said Shin Shira, "as you'll quickly find out if you remain here long. And now—now that you are the possessor of Aladdin's lamp—what are you going to do with it?"

"I—I don't know," I stammered. "I must have time to think."

"I should have diamonds," advised Shin Shira: "they're so easy to carry and can always be converted into money. Command him to bring you a bag full of diamonds of all sizes."

"But, but," I said hesitatingly, as visions of untold wealth floated before my eyes, "will he really do it?"

"Try him and see," said Shin Shira. So I took the lamp in my hand, and rather nervously commanded the Slave to bring me a bag of diamonds.

The Slave fell to the ground and touched his head to the floor, paying me the deepest mark of respect.

"Alas, Master, that it should be so, but you ask your slave that which is impossible, unless you would have me take from the shops that which is not thine."

"Not for worlds," I interrupted. "But how is it that you cannot get me the diamonds from the mines as you used to do for your former Master Aladdin in the olden days?"

A bitter smile spread over the Slave's face.

"The age, Master, has greatly changed, and now the mines in Africa, which were known only to us, are being worked by greedy men with noisy machinery, and we may not be seen there under peril of death. This is the will of the Spirit of the Lamp of whom I am the Slave, and who also calls you Master, though you will never see her."

"Oh, well then, that's all knocked on the head," I said to Shin Shira, who had been listening attentively. "I'll dismiss the man now, shall I, and we'll talk over what's best to be done?"

Shin Shira nodded, so I told the Slave I had no further use for him at the moment, and he vanished.

I stood looking at my little friend in great bewilderment.

"It is a great power to possess," I said, regarding the lamp with awe and amazement. "I hope I shan't do anything foolish with it."

"Don't be silly," said Shin Shira crossly. "I only wish I had your chance. Why, you can do *anything* with a power like that. Leave it to me to think over for to-night, and I'll tell you the best thing to do in the morning."

"But I'm starting for England the first thing to-morrow," I objected.

"Oh! you must put that off for the present," was the decided reply. "I'll be here about eleven, and we'll talk over what's best to be done. Good-night!" and the little fellow held out his hand and strutted off.

I slept very little that night, as you may imagine, and all sorts of vague ideas came into my head as to what I should do with the wonderful power which had so mysteriously come within my grasp.

I had arrived at no definite decision as to what was best to be done, however, by eleven the next morning, when, punctual to the minute, Shin Shira, looking very spruce and alert, knocked at my door.

I noticed with considerable interest that he wore in his turban the diamond which I had so often admired, and he saw me looking at it at once.

"Yes," he said, with a series of little nods, "it was very easy. An hour ago I called on the Chief Magistrate, and found him full of apologies and quite convinced that he had made a grievous mistake. It appears that the original diamond, which Mustapha stole, when found, had some of the gold setting still attached to it, proving beyond doubt that it was the missing jewel, so that my own was returned to me; and the Magistrate even insisted on providing a new aigrette and in having it replaced in my turban by a skilled person. So here it is," and he took off his head-dress and regarded it with considerable pride. "But now to your affairs. I am still in favour of the idea of the diamonds."

"But how—" I began, when Shin Shira interrupted me.

"Are you game for a very exciting adventure?" said he.

"I—don't know." I hesitated. "I seem to have had about enough of exciting adventures."

"It will be something to write about," suggested the Dwarf, "and will undoubtedly make your fortune."

"Well," I said, "what is it? Let's hear."

"Do you remember where Sinbad the Sailor got *his* diamonds from?"

"Yes, of course!" I replied, for I knew my *Arabian Nights* by heart.

"Very well, then," said Shin Shira. "All you've got to do is to get the Slave of the Lamp to bring us the Roc, which I happen to know is still alive; we can then fasten ourselves to his claws, and he will fly back to his home with us, and there, as you know, the ground is strewn with precious stones."

"But why not send the Slave for them?" I argued.

"He evidently doesn't know where they are, and it's as well to keep him ignorant on the subject, in case the lamp passed out of your power, in which case he might use his knowledge in favour of his next master. And, besides, the Roc couldn't carry him there."

"He wouldn't have to," said I. "The Slave evidently has the power of being able to transport himself to any place at will."

"But *we* don't know where to direct him to," said Shin Shira impatiently. He was evidently bent upon carrying out his project, and at last I somewhat weakly consented to his proposal.

I rubbed the lamp and summoned the Slave, who appeared promptly as before.

"I'm sorry to ask such a difficult thing, but can you catch the Roc for me and bring it here?" said I, somewhat apologetically.

"It shall be here, Master, in twenty minutes," replied the Slave imperturbably, vanishing again at a wave from my hand.

"I don't know, I'm sure, what I want diamonds for, when I have such a willing servant," I grumbled, still rather unwilling to venture upon what I regarded as an uncanny undertaking.

"He can't provide you with money," said Shin Shira.

"Why not?" I asked.

"He'd have either to steal it or make it. If he did the latter it wouldn't be legal, and, besides, if it was found out, you might be arrested for circulating unauthorised coin."

"Oh, very well, then, let's go on this wild-goose chase if you're so bent upon it," I said, seeing that he was determined to have his way. A few minutes later we heard a great commotion in the courtyard, and looking from the balcony we saw my Slave carrying by the legs an enormous bird, who turned his head about from side to side, staring stupidly at everything around him. Shin Shira bustled about and got ropes and straps, and with the assistance of the landlord and one or two onlookers, we were soon harnessed in quite an ingenious manner to the claws of our strange steed (if one may call him so).

"His pinions were strong and mighty."

The Slave released him, and the Roc immediately flew slowly up into the air, violently shaking his claws now and then in a vain endeavour to get rid of the unusual weight. Fortunately, however, the straps and ropes, which had been fastened over the bird's back as well, were very strong, and so the worst thing that happened to us was a thorough shaking.

This was of no consequence, and when I realised that I was quite safe, I began actually to enjoy the strange experience of being carried through the air, I knew not whither. In this case, however, the distance was not nearly so great as one might have expected, for leaving the city, the great bird soared over a tract of forest land, above one or two more towns, and so out into the open desert, in the midst of which was a range of rocky mountains. His pinions were strong and mighty, so that he flew very rapidly, and in a little less than two hours he had alighted on a kind of tableland, at the top of one of the mountain peaks, and we were at our journey's end.

There was no doubt but that we were at the right place, for the ground was strewn with stones which, though uncut, sparkled, in the places where they had been chipped or broken, with a hundred different brilliant colours and shades.

Shin Shira drew his knife and quickly cut the ropes and straps which bound us to the now struggling bird, and he was soon released from his uncomfortable burden.

He shook himself once or twice and preened his great feathers, and then stalked off to where an enormous nest could be seen in a cleft in the rocks.

I have no doubt the patient and stupid bird told his mate in bird language what a very strange and uncomfortable experience he had had, and at all events he kept out of our sight from that moment.

Shin Shira at once busied himself by gathering some of the largest gems as quickly as possible; and taking from his pockets some strong linen bags which he had thoughtfully provided, he handed two to me and told me to fill them for myself.

This I did, and also put several into my various pockets. I was just about to say that I thought we had sufficient, when Shin Shira called my attention to a balloon hovering just above our heads.

There were two people in the basket, and they were peering at us over the edge through glasses.

Presently one of them shouted an order, and the balloon quickly descended, so that we could hear the rush of escaping gas as it was being released.

"Hullo there!" shouted a voice over our heads, "who are you? We've never before heard that these mountains were inhabited."

"Neither are they," replied Shin Shira. "We are geologists from Baghdad, and are taking home specimens of the rocks and stones."

"Oh, we're going to Baghdad. Can we give you a lift?" said the voice kindly, and the balloon descended still further, till at last we were able to see the two occupants distinctly.

"It's really very kind of you;—I—I think we will accept your offer," said I, while Shin Shira frowned disapproval.

"Don't go," he whispered, "we can get some more precious stones if we wait a little longer."

"But how are we to get back?" I answered.

"The Magic Lamp," said he.

"Oh, but I've left that behind at the hotel," I replied.

"In that case," said Shin Shira regretfully, "there's nothing else to be done, I suppose."

So we thankfully accepted the aeronauts' kind invitation, and were soon floating comfortably towards Baghdad.

I must confess that it was far more pleasant than the outward journey had been.

Before we got to Baghdad, though, Shin Shira had the misfortune to disappear, much to the horror of the aeronauts, who thought he had fallen out of the basket, and who would scarcely credit my explanation when I told them of Shin Shira's peculiar misfortune in this respect.

He left the two bags of precious stones behind him, and they stood beside mine at the bottom of the basket.

For a few minutes the balloon, being freed from Shin Shira's weight, rapidly ascended, but presently there was a terrible escape of gas and we began to descend again at a great rate.

"Throw out the ballast!" cried one of the aeronauts, and the other, seeing the four bags of what he thought were worthless stones, in his haste and eagerness thrust them overboard.

I was too alarmed at the moment to notice what he was doing, and it was only when matters had been put right, by stopping the escape of gas, that I realised what had happened.

It was useless, however, to cry over spilt milk, and all my thought now was to get back to the hotel in safety.

This we eventually did, and my ballooning friends accepted my invitation to take dinner at the hotel with me, so that after my adventure of the day I had a very pleasant evening. It was not till the next morning that I discovered that Aladdin's Lamp had vanished—had, in fact, probably been stolen.

There was nothing left to do now but to set out for England, which I eventually reached; and on arriving in London, and having the stones which I had brought back in my pockets valued, I found that there were many worthless ones among them, and that the few good ones, when sold, only realised sufficient to pay the rather heavy expenses of my journey to and from Baghdad, with a very little over for myself to repay me for the loss of my time.

* * * * *

MYSTERY NO. VIII

SHIN SHIRA AND THE MAD BULL

The Verrinder children were in a state of great excitement and glee, for we were going to spend the day at Burnham Beeches.

The plan was to drive over in a wagonette and have a picnic under the trees in the middle of the day.

Lionel was amongst the party, and Lady Betty, a young friend of the Verrinders, so that we were a merry crowd as we scrambled into the wagonette.

"It doesn't matter about your being old," said Fidge, snuggling up to me and catching hold of my arm; "you're not like most grown-ups, and don't mind us larking about a bit."

"I hope not," I said smilingly.

"Besides, he isn't old," chimed in Lady Betty, "at least not very," she qualified. "He hasn't even got a beard, and if he wasn't a little bit grown-up he couldn't afford to take us about," she added practically.

"I expect we'll have some jolly decent grub," I heard Dick whisper to Lionel. "Mrs. Putchy makes ripping pastry. I know, because we used to stay at his place sometimes before you came."

Marjorie looked up from her book and smiled and nodded across at me. "It's lovely," she said, as we drove along. "We're going to have a perfectly splendid day."

We were sitting three aside, and there was just comfortable room for us; and when we had got well into the country I began to tell the younger ones, Fidge and Lady Betty, a story. Marjorie closed her book too and leaned forward to listen, but the two big boys, evidently considering it *infra dig.* to listen to anything so childish, were eagerly comparing school experiences. Dick was at Harrow and Lionel at Marlborough, so they had a lot to talk about.

Presently, in the middle of my story, Marjorie called out, without looking up, "Move further along, Dick, don't crowd so."

"I'm not!" retorted Dick, "it's you. I can't move any further without crowding Lionel out of the trap."

"Oh, it's this cushion," cried Marjorie, turning about and trying to remove what looked at first like a yellow silk cushion beside her.

It was evidently too heavy though, and she gave a start as she touched it. "Why!" she exclaimed, "it's got something alive in it!"

We all turned around to see what she meant, and at once I knew that it was Shin Shira appearing.

"Oh, jolly!" cried all the children but Lionel, when I explained to them what was happening.

"It's all very well, and he's good fun and all that," said my young cousin, "but if you'd had the experience that I had with his old Magic Carpet, you'd be very careful not to have much to do with him—he's rather dangerous."

"But think of the adventures you have with him," said Dick enviously. "I wouldn't funk it if he asked me to go anywhere with him."

"Who's funking it?" demanded Lionel angrily.

"Well, *you* didn't seem to have much desire to repeat your experiences, my friend," laughed Shin Shira. "My head and ears just happened to arrive in time for me to gather that."

Lionel turned very red. "Oh well, sir, I did have rather a rough time on the Magic Carpet, you know."

"So you did, so you did," agreed Shin Shira, amiably beaming on us all. "And where may all you young people be off to this fine day?"

"We're having a picnic," said Lady Betty shyly.

"Going to have, you mean," corrected Fidge. "It isn't a picnic till you begin to eat, you know."

"Would you mind if I joined you?" asked the Yellow Dwarf, appealing to me.

"Well, it strikes me that you have done so," I laughed; "but we shall be delighted with your company if you care to stay."

"That's all right then," said Shin Shira, settling down comfortably; "there's nothing I should like better this warm day," and he took off his turban and rubbed his little bald head with a yellow silk handkerchief.

The sight of the jewel in it reminded him to ask me what became of the two bags of diamonds he left in the basket of the balloon when he disappeared on our way back to Baghdad.

I told him what had happened, and how I had lost all of mine except the few almost worthless ones which I had put in my pocket.

"I was rather more fortunate," said Shin Shira, "for amongst those which I saved were one or two very valuable ones, and several more which I can sell at a very good price when it becomes necessary."

"But I thought you could have whatever you wished for?" said Dick.

"Oh no," replied the Dwarf, "not money, you know—almost anything else, but not money, because, you see, it wouldn't be legal to make money, and I can tell you I have often found it very awkward to have appeared in a strange place with no money at all in my pocket. I have indeed once or twice almost been tempted to sell even the jewel which the Princess gave me. Now fortunately that will never be necessary."

"What part of Burnham Beeches do you wish me to drive to, sir?" asked the coachman at this moment; "we're just coming to the village."

"Oh, you'd better put the horses up at the stables, and get a man to help you with the hampers, and we'll walk on to the wood. You know where I generally have luncheon."

"Very well, sir!" said the man, touching his hat with his whip and stopping at the old-fashioned inn in the village.

We were all very glad to stretch our legs after the long ride, and having had some lemonade and fruit at a little shop in the High Street, we quite enjoyed the walk up to the wood.

Here under the trees in a beautiful spot we sat down to wait for the men with the hampers.

After waiting for some time with growing impatience, our coachman turned up with a rueful face.

"There ain't no hamper, sir," he said.

"What?" I exclaimed. "No hamper! What do you mean?"

"There ain't no hamper in the trap, sir. I didn't have it up in front, so I thought you had it in with you. Do you think it's fallen out, sir?"

"By Jove, sir!" cried Lionel suddenly, "it's my fault. You told me to see that the man put the hampers on in front, and I clean forgot all about it."

If it hadn't been such a serious matter it would have been highly amusing to watch the blank dismay depicted on every face on hearing this disastrous news.

"What on earth are we to do?" exclaimed Dick, with almost tragic concern.

"There's only one thing to be done, I suppose," said I resignedly, after sending the man away; "we shall have to return to the village and have our luncheon at the inn."

"It won't be a picnic at all then," pouted Lady Betty ruefully.

Shin Shira was the only one who did not seem distressed about the matter. He had seated himself cross-legged on the ground under one of the old Beeches, and was slowly turning over the leaves of the little yellow book fastened to his belt with a golden chain, which he always wore.

"I think I can be of some assistance to you here," said he, getting up after a time and coming towards me. "Has anybody some paper and a pencil?"

This seemed a strange request at such a moment, but between us we managed to find what he asked for.

The Dwarf suddenly tore the paper into seven parts, handing us each one and keeping one for himself.

"Now," said he, "each of you write on the piece of paper the name of something you would wish for luncheon."

He handed me the pencil first, and just for fun I wrote "Lobster salad."

Marjorie wrote "Game pie."

Dick thought that "Pies and tarts and plenty of them" was a suitable thing to ask for.

Lionel could imagine nothing more to be desired than "Ham and tongue sandwiches."

Lady Betty wanted "Fruit and nuts," and Fidge, after various painful attempts, wrote "Something nice to drink."

Shin Shira read them out one by one.

"Yes," he said, "they're all very well, but how are you going to eat them when you have got them? Now you see what I wish for," and he carefully wrote on his slip of paper, "Tablecloth, serviettes, plates, dishes, knives, forks, spoons, salt, pepper, mustard, oil, vinegar, glasses and a corkscrew." "There!" he exclaimed, "I think that will put us right. Now watch carefully. You see there is no deception!" and he laughingly rolled up his sleeves like a professional conjurer.

He placed the paper upon which he had written his list into his turban, shaking it violently.

To our surprise, in a few seconds it sounded as though there was something in it, and an instant later he drew forth from it a neatly folded snow-white tablecloth, the serviettes, spoons, forks, and in fact all the articles which he had named.

He set the children to work laying the cloth, while he placed the other lists in his turban, and in turn, beginning with a deliciously fresh-looking lobster salad, and a large game pie, he brought forth every one of the good things which had been wished for.

Fidge's "something nice to drink" turned out to be bottles of lemonade, milk, soda water, and a bottle of wine for the grown-ups.

A more delicious feast it would be impossible to imagine.

We were just sitting down to enjoy it, and I had stuck the knife and fork into the game pie, when Marjorie sprang up with a little scream, brushing something from her face.

"Ough! a horrid caterpillar!" she cried.

"And here's another!" declared Fidge, knocking one from his coat.

"And an earwig!" exclaimed Dick, picking one up from the cloth.

"Oh! and spiders!" screamed Lady Betty, jumping up and shaking her frock.

"Dear! dear! this will never do!" I said, for the place was swarming with insects, owing to the very dry summer which we had had.

"There ought to be a marquee like we had at the choir treat," said Fidge.

"Oh, I vote we get on with the grub," said Dick greedily. "The insects won't kill us."

"No, but a marquee would certainly be more comfortable," said Shin Shira. "Come into the meadow just over there, and I'll see if I can provide one."

Leaving Lionel to guard our feast, the rest of us all trailed after him, over the fence into the meadow, which was carpeted with soft long grass.

"The only thing is, I can't exactly remember what a marquee is like," he said. "Think, my dear boy, what the one was like which you had in your mind."

"Why, it had four poles, one at each corner," said Fidge, "and some iron things connecting them at the top, and it was covered all over and round the sides with some stripey stuff. Then there were ropes and things, and pegs driven into the ground to tie the poles to, and a trestle table and two long forms each side. That's all. Oh, yes, and Piggott & Son, Tentmakers, was written in big letters on the stripey stuff."

"Ah!" said Shin Shira, "I think I shall be able to imagine it sufficiently well now. I'll try," and after consulting his little yellow book again for instructions, he called for a stick, which the boys soon cut from the hedge, and marked out a large square space in the meadow; and then, using some magic words, he waved the stick three times, and there stood the very marquee which Fidge had described, even to the words Piggott & Son, Tentmakers, on the canvas covering.

"Now go and bring the luncheon, children, and we'll try again," said Shin Shira, in a rare good humour with himself (the little fellow was evidently delighted to find that his fairy powers were acting so well to-day); and soon we were seated around the table, which, I must confess, I found a more comfortable way of enjoying my luncheon.

To say that we did full justice to the good things provided, is but mildly describing the way the food disappeared.

The two elder boys in particular seemed as though they would never leave off, but at last we settled down comfortably to the fruit and nuts, and were just discussing what we should do with the marquee and its contents, when we suddenly all started to our feet in alarm.

A loud bellowing, combined with a dull sound of galloping hoofs, told us that something was coming our way.

I rushed to the door and looked out.

"Good heavens! A mad bull!" I cried, "tearing this way at a furious pace."

Shin Shira sprang to the opening.

"I'll attract him in another direction, and while he is after me you all escape over the fence," he cried hurriedly, and snatching a red silk handkerchief from Lionel's pocket, he rushed out into the open.

The bull paused, and though I frantically shouted to Shin Shira to come back, the brave little fellow flourished the red handkerchief to attract the creature's attention. With a bellow of anger the infuriated animal, holding his head down, tore after the Dwarf, who ran with surprising swiftness in the opposite direction to the marquee.

"Now children, quickly!" I cried, catching Lady Betty by the hand, and we all made for the fence as quickly as possible.

We were no sooner in safety than we turned to see how our gallant little friend was faring.

The yellow figure, still waving the red handkerchief, was running ahead of the bull, but to our great distress we could see that the beast was gaining on him.

"Oh dear! he'll never reach the other side in time," cried Marjorie, hiding her eyes in her hands and sinking to the ground in a panic of fear and fright.

Presently the boys gave an excited shout—"Hurrah! Bravo!" they cried, jumping from the fence and skipping about, tossing their caps into the air in an excess of relief. I sat down beside Marjorie and explained to her what had happened.

The bull was rapidly gaining on Shin Shira and the little fellow was becoming exhausted, when, by a happy chance, at that very moment he began to disappear, and before the bull could reach him he had vanished altogether.

The bull was rushing frantically about, bellowing and snorting and looking in vain for him, and at last, turning his attention to the marquee, he dashed into it, ripping up the canvas and overturning the table, smashing the dishes, and altogether making a most terrific commotion.

Now that we were all safe we could make light of the loss of the marquee and its contents, and could even smile at the quaint remark of Lady Betty when she said solemnly—

"In future I shall prefer to picnic where there are spiders, instead of where mad bulls are about. In fact, I shall rather like spiders after this: they're so gentle and don't bellow at all."

The boys were still watching the havoc which the bull was creating, when they noticed a man walking towards us beside the fence.

He was a big, burly farmer and looked very angry.

"Now then," he cried, in a surly voice, "what do you mean by all this?"

"I don't understand you," I answered.

"I speak plain English, don't I?" he said. "Wasn't it you that's been trampling in my long grass, and building tents and what not on private property? I'll learn you that I won't have no strangers in my meadows, I can tell ye."

"I'm very sorry if I've done any harm," said I, "and I'm sure if—"

"*If* you've done any harm!" shouted the farmer. "Look at all that long grass trampled down all over the meadow."

"Yes," I interrupted, "but it was your bull which did that."

"He wouldn't have done it if you hadn't teased him," said the farmer obstinately. "I saw one of you myself teasing him with a red rag and making him furious. I'm not going to have any of it. Off you come with me to the police station."

"No, no, I can't do that," I cried in alarm; "I have these children with me."

"People shouldn't take children out if they can't do without getting into mischief," grumbled the farmer. "No, you come along of me," and he caught hold of my arm.

"I'll give you my card," I said, "and if you have any serious complaint to make you can write to me."

"Aye, a likely story; and when I write to you, as likely as not I'll find you've given me a wrong address."

"Come back with me then to the inn: they know me there and will tell you whether or no the address is a correct one."

The old farmer was gradually persuaded to this course, though he grumbled all the way there that I ought to be "locked up," while the children, thoroughly subdued, walked in silence behind us.

"You'll have to pay a pretty penny for damages," said he warningly, when he had satisfied himself at the inn that I was known as "a gentleman who often drove over there in the summer, and always paid for what he had."

I assured him that he should have what was just, and when he had gone I ordered tea in the arbour at the end of the old-fashioned garden, and over it we forgot the unfortunate, but exciting, termination to our picnic.

We arrived home quite safely. Sure enough, a few days afterwards I received a preposterous claim for damage to the farmer's grass, which I left my solicitor to deal with; and more extraordinary still, I had a claim from Messrs. Piggott & Son for damages to a tent, which they "could not trace as having been hired to me, but which I must have hired at some time or another, since it bore their name marked as they only marked their tents let out on hire."

This letter also went to my solicitor, and to this day I've heard nothing further about either matter.

* * * * *

MYSTERY NO. IX

SHIN SHIRA AND THE QUEEN OF HEARTS

It was many months after this last adventure before I saw my friend Shin Shira again.

The summer was past, and it was the time of fires and warm drawn curtains. One evening, after dinner, I was sitting alone in my study, puzzling over a chess problem, when the servant brought me a card on which I read—

"Dr. Shin Shira Scaramanga Manousa Yama Hawa."

"Oh!" I laughed, "show him in at once, please." For I had been longing for an opportunity of thanking the gallant little fellow for the bravery he had shown in the matter of the mad bull—a bravery to which some of us, at all events, probably owed our lives.

"Come in, come in! Delighted to see you!" I cried, getting up and making him comfortable in "the Toad," the chair which I know he likes best. I got out the tobacco jar, and we were soon chatting comfortably over our pipes.

"By the way," I said, picking up his card again and looking at it, when we had exhausted most of the topics of conversation which came to our minds, "I didn't know before that you were a doctor."

"Oh, I don't practise, and I seldom use the title except on my cards. It was given to me by the King of Hearts very many years ago. Ha-ha-ha!" And Shin Shira laughed heartily at what was evidently a humorous recollection.

"Won't you tell me about it, please?" said I.

"I don't know," replied the Dwarf, "that there is much to tell.

"It was while I was travelling round the world in my earlier days, and I had come, in the course of my wanderings, upon the country ruled over by the King of Hearts and his most charming Queen.

"Talk about turtle-doves! I had never seen such a perfectly devoted couple before in my life. They were like a pair of happy lovers, although they must have been married several years before I knew them.

"I happened to appear at their Majesties' dinner-table one evening when they were dining alone, just as dinner was being served.

"Of course they were greatly astonished at seeing me suddenly appear in their presence, especially as I arrived at a particularly awkward moment, when, the servants being busy with the dishes and having their backs turned, the King was squeezing her Majesty's hand under the table, and looking lovingly into her eyes.

"The King turned to the Lord Chief Butler, when that official returned, and looking at me curiously, said, 'It's very thoughtless of me, but I do not remember that I invited any guests for this evening.'

"'I had heard nothing of it either, your Majesty,' said the Lord Chief Butler, pursing up his lips and looking at me severely. 'Shall I request the Lord High Footman and the Lord Under Footman to remove the person?'

"'By no means,' said the King kindly; 'I will ask him myself what brings him here.'

"'It was a matter of compulsion, rather than of inclination, your Majesty,' said I. And I explained as well as I was able the curious affliction from which I suffer, of having to appear and disappear at the fairies' pleasure.

"'Most interesting—most!' said the Queen, smiling sweetly, 'and we should be most inhospitable if we did not make you welcome here for so long as the fairies will spare you to us.'

"This gracious speech, and the Queen's beauty, quite won my heart, and putting my hand on my heart, I bowed in the most graceful manner that I could command.

"The Lord Chief Butler, seeing that I was in favour with their Majesties, now brought me a plate, and some glasses, and waited upon me most obsequiously.

"'Tarts, my lord!' he announced, handing me a silver dish on which were piled some rather stodgy-looking jam affairs.

"'No thank you,' I replied.

"The man looked horrified, and the King and Queen greatly embarrassed by my refusal. 'Er—tarts—er—your Highness,—er—her Majesty's own make,' whispered the Lord Chief Butler.

"'Oh, then by all means I will change my mind,' said I gallantly, and I took two of the tarts on my plate, while the King and Queen looked on approvingly.

"I can safely say that in all my wanderings, through all these years, I have never before or since tasted such exceedingly unpleasant tarts.

"I hesitate to say more, out of respect to the most beautiful and gracious Queen who ever lived, but I could say a great deal.

"However, I managed to get through them, even to the bitter end, and had the satisfaction of seeing her Majesty look greatly delighted.

"'I really must have another one, my love,' declared the King; 'they are most delicious, made as they were by your own royal and beautiful hands.'

"'No—no—dearest,' smiled the Queen, her pride in her pastry battling with her consideration for her husband's health, 'you have already had two.'

"'Perhaps, my darling, you are right,' replied the King, with a sigh of relief, and hurriedly motioning to the Lord Chief Butler to remove his plate.

"'Perhaps our guest, though—' began the Queen sweetly.

"'No—no—thank you, your Majesty,' I hastened to say. 'I never—*never*—by any chance indulge in more than two, under doctor's strict orders.'

"'Very well then,' said her Majesty, 'we will have dessert.'

"The rest of the dinner was uneventful, and I was more and more impressed as the time went on with the gracious and simple bearing of the exalted personages of whom I was an uninvited guest.

"At last her Majesty rose, gave me a bow, and was led with old-fashioned courtesy by his Majesty to the door, which was thrown open by the servants, and the King and I were left alone to our coffee and cigars. After we had talked on various subjects for some time, I ventured to express my admiration of, and devotion to, the gracious lady who had just left us, and the King's eyes sparkled with delight.

"'You may well admire her, sir; she is rightly beloved for her graciousness and beauty from one end of my kingdom to the other, and her thoughtfulness and kindness to myself are beyond expression.

"'I *must* tell you of a little incident (which you have just shared in) to prove to you how wholly devoted she is to my interests.

"'I have, as many other royal personages have at times, some difficulty in regulating my affairs so as to make both ends meet comfortably.

"'Her Majesty knew of this, and immediately began to take cooking lessons with a view to cooking for us when we are alone, and thus saving expenses in the kitchen. The tarts you tasted to-day are her Majesty's first attempt.'

"'R-eally!' I murmured, seeing that the King paused as though he expected me to say something.

"'Yes,' continued his Majesty, 'and to-morrow she has made me promise to catch her some blackbirds, with which to make a pie.'

"'Catch them?' I cried; 'why not shoot them?'

"'Oh! the Queen wouldn't think of letting me do anything so cruel, she is *so* tender-hearted. But you'll come with me to-morrow, and help me to catch some, won't you?'

"I assured his Majesty that unless I had unfortunately to disappear before then, I should be delighted, and we went up to join her Majesty in the drawing-room.

"We found the Queen surrounded by her Maids of Honour, of whom some were sitting at the tambour frames, others doing fine embroidery, while two of their number were at the piano playing and singing.

"I was presented to these ladies, and, at the Queen's request, related some of the extraordinary adventures which, as you know, have, at one time or another in my long career, befallen me. The evening was quite a success, and I felt that I had indeed fallen upon my feet in such charming company.

"At a moderately early hour we retired, and in the morning, soon after breakfast, his Majesty and I started on our expedition in quest of blackbirds for the Queen's pie.

"Her Majesty and the Maids of Honour watched us start off from the balcony, and several retainers followed at a respectful distance, carrying various bags and implements of which I could not even imagine the uses.

"When we had got some distance from the Castle, his Majesty whispered to me confidentially that he must confess that he didn't know much about this sort of thing.

"'Er—do you recommend—er—*salt* for blackbirds?' he inquired anxiously.

"'What for?' I asked.

"'To put on their tails, you know,' said the King. 'I have a recollection of hearing something, somewhere, about catching birds by putting salt on their tails. But perhaps that doesn't refer to blackbirds?' he added.

"I couldn't help smiling a little at the simple, good-natured, inexperienced King, but suggested immediately afterwards that some grain scattered before and inside a sieve propped up with a stick, to which some string was attached, would probably be a more effectual way of catching the birds.

"'What a brilliant idea!' said the King. 'I'll send the salt back and order some sieves, grain, sticks and string, as you suggest. Is there anything else?'

"'Something to put the birds in if we catch any, your Majesty,' said I. "'Oh! I've thought of that,' said the King, 'and have several baskets ready.'

"The men were soon back with the sieves, and I quickly rigged up two of them as traps; and having baited them, I showed the King how to hide and pull the string directly one of the birds was under the sieve.

"Fortunately, blackbirds seemed to abound in that country, and there were soon several fluttering about, pecking at and picking up the grain.

"Presently, one got under my sieve, and pulling the support away by the string, I was fortunate enough to catch it. The King was delighted, and the more so when a few minutes afterwards he trapped two at once, in the same manner.

"After this, the 'sport,' if it could be called so, became fast and furious, and ended in our catching four-and-twenty birds between us.

"This the King considered would be sufficient, so we set off to the Castle again, the men bearing the baskets in triumph before us.

"'Oh! the dear, sweet little things!' cried Her Majesty, when she was shown our captives, 'and how clever of you to have caught them all! They'll make a perfectly lovely pie!' And she set off in high glee to the kitchens, to try her hand at the culinary art again.

"This was carefully set before the King."

"The afternoon was spent in the beautiful gardens surrounding the Castle, playing fives, for which there was a specially built court, and practising at archery, so that the time quickly passed, till we were called in by the first dinner gong.

"The Maids of Honour, together with some of the State Ministers, joined us at dinner, and I could see that the Queen, though sweet and gracious as ever, was very anxious as the dinner proceeded.

"Presently there was a flourish of trumpets heard at the door, and two pages appeared, bearing a silver salver upon which was an enormous pie. This was carefully set before the King, and his Majesty, after smiling at the Queen rather nervously, put the knife into the crust and removed a portion of it.

"Immediately afterwards, there was a great commotion heard from inside the pie, and first one bird and then another began to sing, hopping out of the pie and on to the table, evidently delighted at regaining its liberty.

"Finally, amid the breathless silence of all about the table, they flew off through the open window, and nothing was left but the crust.

"The Queen sat back in her chair looking half-triumphant and half-ashamed.

"'I'm afraid it isn't a very satisfactory pie, from the eating point of view,' she faltered, 'but I *couldn't* have the poor pretty little things killed, and so I put them in the dish alive, and when the crust, which I baked separately, was nearly cold, I cut a hole in the top, so that they could breathe, and put it over them.'

"'It does your heart much credit, my love,' cried the King, 'and, the thought of cutting a hole in the crust was a very kind one.'

"And indeed, wherever and in whatever country I have been since that time, many years ago, and have related the story, the ladies of that country have always made a hole in the top of their pies, in honour of the beautiful and kind Queen who first invented it.

"I did not hear much more of the conversation which followed this episode, for unfortunately, just then, I felt myself disappearing, and had only just time to incline my head respectfully to the King and Queen before I had vanished."

"But," I remarked, when Shin Shira left off speaking, "you haven't told me yet how you came to get the title of 'Doctor.'"

"Oh, that's all part of the same story," said Shin Shira, refilling his pipe; "it has a sequel. About seven months after the events which I have narrated" (you'll have noticed that Shin Shira loved using long words when he could), "I found myself again in the same country, and I thought I could not leave it without paying my respects to the amiable King and Queen; so, one fine afternoon, I made my way up to the Castle.

"I found the King in his counting-house, industriously counting out his money. He left off when he saw me, though, and came forward to greet me heartily.

"'The Queen, bless her! will be as delighted to see you as I am,' said he; 'we'll go and find her. I fancy I know where she is.'

"He led the way at once to the parlour, and there we found her Majesty looking sweet and amiable as ever.

"She was rather confused at being discovered in the act of eating some bread and honey.

"'I am suffering from a very poor appetite,' her Majesty explained, after she had made me welcome, 'and have eaten nothing at all to-day, and just now I fancied a little honey, for which I have a great liking.'

"'I hope your Majesty is not unwell, that your appetite is so feeble?' I inquired with great solicitation.

"'Oh no!' replied the Queen, with an effort at brightness; 'I'm a little worried, that's all.'

"'We're all worried, more or less,' chimed in the King. '*You* remember that blackbird pie, don't you?'

"'Yes, your Majesty, of course I do,' said I, smiling at the recollection.

"'Well, those birds, the ones which were put into it, have become very spiteful and dangerous. They have taken to haunting the precincts of the Castle, and attack the servants when they go into the garden, particularly the laundry maids; for, when they go into the garden to hang out the clothes, they have to use both hands to do so, and then these wretched birds fly down and peck at their noses. One poor creature lost hers altogether, with the result that all of the maids have given notice, and we can't get laundry maids for love or money.'

"'It's very trying,' said the Queen; 'the poor King has to wear his things much longer than he should, and I have a difficulty in even getting a clean pocket-handkerchief.'

"It was a curious difficulty to be in, certainly, and I felt very anxious to help them if I could, so I asked permission to be allowed to visit the servants' hall, and talk to the maids on the subject.

"This was readily given, and I spoke to them as earnestly as I could about their good Queen and mistress, and how willing and eager they ought to be to do everything they could for her.

"I could see that they felt this keenly themselves, for some of them were in tears when I spoke of the Queen's goodness to everybody about her.

"'B—but our precious noses, sir!' sobbed one good-natured girl; 'we can't afford to lose them, can we now?'

"'No,' I said, 'but I have thought of a way by which it will be quite safe for you to go into the garden.

"'Now, like good creatures, the first thing in the morning, set to and get some laundry work done, and I'll go out and hang up some of the clothes, and you'll see that the birds won't hurt me.'

"They all agreed to this, and the good-natured girl who had been crying said, 'I'll come with you, if you like, and show you how to hang the things up.'

"'So you shall,' said I, and went up to my room to make preparations for the morning.

"It was quite simple. I sent for some coloured wax, and having made a wooden model of a nose, I made on it some little waxen cases which could be worn over one's own nose, and *then*, if the birds pecked at it, it wouldn't matter in the least.

"In the morning, the wax cases were quite set and hard, and when the maid and I went out to hang up the clothes, it was great fun to see the bewilderment of a large blackbird when he flew away with the maid's false nose, and she calmly stuck on another.

"The birds soon gave up their evil ways after that, but for some months, as a precaution, the maids never ventured out without a nose protector.

"It was for this useful invention that the King of Hearts bestowed on me the title of 'Doctor to His Majesty's Household.'"

"H'm!" I remarked, when he had finished, "it's a very remarkable story. I seem to have heard of some of the incidents before, somehow."

"Very likely, very likely," said Shin Shira "Well, I must be going now." And he shook hands and went out by the door, in a sensible way for once.

As he went out of the house, I heard him singing softly—

> "The Queen of Hearts, she made some tarts
>   All on a summer's day"—

And then he changed his song to—

> "Sing a song of sixpence,
>   A pocketful of rye,

>   Four-and-twenty blackbirds
>   Baked in a pie.
>
>   The maid was in the garden
>   Hanging out the clothes,
>   And along came a blackbird
>   And nipped off her nose."

And I remembered then why his story had seemed so familiar.

* * * * *

MYSTERY NO. X AND LAST

SHIN SHIRA DISAPPEARS

The day after my little friend had related to me his experiences in the land of the King and Queen of Hearts, I was surprised to receive a portmanteau addressed to me, which, on my opening it, I found to contain the little yellow costume, including the turban with the diamond ornament, which Shin Shira had always worn.

There was no note enclosed, and I naturally wondered very much what had occasioned this strange parcel being sent to me.

I had no means of communicating with Shin Shira, and so had to wait with what patience I could summon for an explanation from him.

I had not long to wait, fortunately, for in the afternoon of the same day the little fellow burst in upon me, clothed in a frock coat, tall hat and regulation costume of a gentleman in easy circumstances.

I must say he was not nearly such a picturesque looking person as he had been in his Oriental dress. He threw himself into a chair and seemed overflowing with news.

"I've decided to settle down," he said breathlessly. "I didn't tell you yesterday because my arrangements were not quite completed, but I've begun now, and I'm going to settle down."

"What *do* you mean?" I inquired, utterly bewildered by my friend's abrupt statement.

"Why," he began, "I'm tired of this constant changing from one place to another; and as I've not had to disappear now for some time, I've come to the conclusion that the fairies have overlooked the misdeeds of my ancestors and are going to give me a rest. I've taken a house in the highly respectable neighbourhood of Russell Square, and I've furnished it by means of my fairy powers with everything that is necessary; besides this, I've realised the full value of all my precious stones, except, of course, that which the dear Princess gave me, and have opened a banking account. There!" and the little fellow sat back, evidently feeling quite exhausted by his long speech and vainly searching for his little fan, which, of course, was not there.

I scarcely knew what to say to this surprising statement, and waited for further developments before replying. "I've engaged a housekeeper to look after me, and two servants also; and—as you see—have discarded my Oriental costume for one more suitable to this country and climate; I sent you my old costume and turban by a trustworthy messenger this morning, having changed at my tailor's into the attire in which you see me. I hope it has arrived safely?"

I assured him that it had, and sent for the portmanteau in order that he might see for himself.

"That's all right, then," he said with a sigh of relief; "and now I want to hand you this blank cheque which I have signed, and, in case I disappear, I want you to draw out the whole amount standing to my account at the bank at the time, so that I may be able to get it in case I appear again. I have an idea that I shall not have to undergo these changes many more times. Of course, if I never come back, the money will be yours, as I have no one else to leave it to."

I thanked him very heartily for the trust he reposed in me, and assured him that his wishes should be carried out to the letter.

"That's all right, then!" he exclaimed in a tone of satisfaction; "and now I want to arrange for a nice little party at my new home to act as a kind of—er—home warming—I think you call it. Ask the children and any of your friends who know me, and, if you let me know beforehand how many are coming, I will arrange for what, I hope, will turn out to be a very enjoyable evening."

We fixed the date, and after my little friend had gone, I wrote informally, as Shin Shira wished, to as many of my friends as would be likely to wish to come, to ask them to attend.

Nearly everybody accepted—for the little fellow was a great favourite with everybody who knew him—and, as Shin Shira looked in every day to know how the replies were coming in, I was able to tell him in a few days that we might expect from twenty to twenty-five guests.

From then till the date fixed Shin Shira was very busy, and I only saw him once or twice, and on the eventful day I did not see him at all.

The Verrinder children were coming in the carriage with me, and, according to arrangement, we were the first to arrive.

There was an awning at the door and a red carpet laid down the steps and across the pavement; the house was brilliantly lighted, and evidently grand preparations had been going on.

I hurried up the steps, followed by Marjorie, Dick and Fidge.

The servant who stood at the open door, and who knew me by sight, was looking very anxious, and whispered, "The housekeeper would like to speak to you at once in the dining-room, sir."

"Anything the matter?" I asked.

"Yes, sir, the master—he—he can't be found," said the man.

I hurried down to the dining-room, and found the housekeeper in her best black silk dress, looking even more distressed than the manservant had been.

"The master, sir," she began at once when I entered the room. "Whatever *is* to be done? He can't be found anywhere—and the guests beginning to arrive—"

"Never mind," said I, after thinking a moment. "I've no doubt he'll be here presently—and, in the meantime, as I know most if not all of the guests, I'll receive them, and explain that he has probably been called away and will no doubt be back presently."

I hurried up into the drawing-room, and found that by this time several guests had arrived, and were looking greatly surprised at finding no host to receive them.

I apologised for my friend as well as I was able, and pointed out that probably he would soon return, and, in the meantime, he would doubtless wish us to make ourselves at home.

We found everything arranged for our comfort. Professional singers gave an excellent concert in the drawing-room—an excellent supper was served downstairs.

The children were not forgotten, and, while the concert had been proceeding in the drawing-room, an amusing entertainment was provided for them in another room. Beside each plate at supper, also, there was a little present, chosen carefully, and our names written distinctly on each.

Everything was thoroughly well thought out and provided for—but—there was no host to receive our thanks and to bid us "good-bye" when we went.

The whole affair, therefore, though I naturally did my best for my friend's sake to "keep things going," concluded rather flatly, and I went home after it was all over feeling not a little depressed and anxious.

I called the next day, and the day after, but Shin Shira had not returned, nor had anything been heard of, or from him.

It was most mysterious, and I could only account for it by the fact that the fairies may have, in fact *must* have, caused him to disappear once more.

The housekeeper told me, on my inquiring of her, that he had been at home the whole of the day on which the party had been held, superintending all the arrangements, and had gone up early to his room to dress, and from that time all trace of him had been lost.

I was very sorry, and the more so as days and weeks flew by and nothing happened to give us any clue as to his whereabouts.

After a couple of months, I told the servants that they had better seek other situations, and when they had done so I let them go. I closed the house, and waited for events.

It must have been quite a year later when I received the following letter—

"*Isle of San Sosta,*
"*South Pacific.*
"My dear Friend,

"I write once more to let you know that I am again in great trouble, but this time there is nothing in which you can help me, though I know, in the goodness of your heart, you would wish to do so if it were possible.

"When, in accordance with the fairies' decree, to which I must always most humbly bow, I was called upon to disappear at the very moment when I was hoping to welcome my guests to my newly established home, I found myself most unexpectedly in this place.

"It is an island very little known, and far out of the beaten track of vessels.

"Once a year, however, a trader calls, bringing and taking letters and exchanging for the produce of this place such necessities as we require from more civilised lands.

"The people of this country are very simple and of primitive habits, so much so that it is the custom here if a maiden remains unmarried after a certain age, and becomes a burden to her parents, to turn her out of the community, and leave her to seek food for herself or starve in the desert.

"This cruel and unnatural law I have constantly tried to get altered, and the King and his advisers consent to do so only on one condition, and that is, that I find a husband for the only unmarried daughter of the King, who is at present an outcast in the wilderness, being of most uncomely appearance and greatly deformed.

"I have been out into the wilderness to see the poor creature myself. She is indeed in a pitiful plight, being far from fair to look upon, and gaunt and thin with exposure and suffering.

"I conversed with her and found her intelligent, and patient under her great afflictions; in fact, her sad case so touched my heart that, not only for her sake, but for the sake of the other unfortunate maidens who, unless this cruel law is altered, may have to suffer a fate similar to hers, I have decided to marry her myself, and thus rescue her and others who may follow her.

"I think of my sweet Princess and feel that she would approve—for never shall I see her dear face again—and in making this marriage she would know I was inclined to it from pity and not from any untruthfulness to her most dear memory.

"The stone she gave me I cannot bear to see any more, and this I ask you to keep *until I claim it again*; all my other goods and the money in the bank I leave to you absolutely.

"I feel that I may never see you again, and if this be so, accept my hearty and devoted thanks for all you have done for me. Think of me sometimes and

"Believe me to be,
"Your friend always,
"Shin Shira Scaramanga Manousa Yama Hawa."

I sat a long while after I had read this letter, thinking of all the strange happenings since I had known my little friend.

I had grown quite to love and respect him, and when I thought of the noble and chivalrous deed he intended performing in order to save the poor creature in that far-off island, I felt that he was indeed worthy of all admiration.

I got down a map, and tried in vain to find the island he mentioned. It was not marked in any of those which I had by me.

Then I found the portmanteau which Shin Shira had left with me, and looked at the little yellow costume, which reminded me so much of my friend.

In lifting it from the bag, something heavy dropped from between the folds. It was the Magic Crystal. I held it in my hand, and wished I could see what Shin Shira was doing at that moment. The thought had no sooner entered my head than I gave an exclamation of surprise.

A mist in which vague figures were moving filled the crystal, and presently I could see distinctly a large crowd of people gathered together. A man and woman stood beneath a canopy—the man I soon perceived was Shin Shira himself, still clothed in the immaculate frock coat and tall hat in which I had last seen him dressed. The woman was a poor, deformed thing and pitifully plain—her gaudy dress and many jewels but helped to point the contrast.

Before them stood a priest, and at the side the King, surrounded by his warriors. It was evidently the celebration of a wedding, and the ceremony was over, for the bridegroom led the bride from under the canopy and knelt with her before the King, who stretched out his hands as though he were giving them his blessing—and then, to my astonishment, a most marvellous thing happened. A blaze of light flashed across the scene, and a beautiful being, who I am convinced was the Fairy Queen herself, floated down from the heights above, accompanied by a crowd of beings nearly as beautiful as herself. She waved her wand three times, and the bride became a beautiful Princess, and Shin Shira grew tall, young and handsome in an instant.

The King and his court gazed in amazement at the scene, and the Princess fell into Shin Shira's arms.

The Fairy waved her wand again, and a bright crown appeared on Shin Shira's head, in which flashed a single stone of great brilliancy. At the same instant the jewel vanished from the yellow turban beside me.

The crystal grew clear as the beautiful scene faded away, and that was the last glimpse I ever had of my little friend.

I often think of him, and I like to imagine, as, indeed, I believe to be the case, that the fairies have restored to him his full powers, and that the bride he had so unselfishly wedded turned out to be the very Princess to whom he had been faithful throughout his long life.

It may be so—if the crystal spoke truly. Who knows?

THE END

BIBLIOBAZAAR

The essential book market!

Did you know that you can get any of our titles in large print?

Did you know that we have an ever-growing collection of books in many languages?

**Order online:
www.bibliobazaar.com**

Find all of your favorite classic books!

Stay up to date with the latest government reports!

At BiblioBazaar, we aim to make knowledge more accessible by making thousands of titles available to you- *quickly and affordably*.

Contact us:
BiblioBazaar
PO Box 21206
Charleston, SC 29413

Printed in Great Britain by
Amazon.co.uk, Ltd.,
Marston Gate.